MERMAIDS SIRENS & CREATURES OF THE WATERS

First published in Great Britain in 2026 by Godsfield Press, an imprint of
Octopus Publishing Group Ltd
Carmelite House
50 Victoria Embankment
London EC4Y 0DZ
www.octopusbooks.co.uk

An Hachette UK Company
www.hachette.co.uk

The authorized representative in the EEA is Hachette Ireland,
8 Castlecourt Centre, Dublin 15, D15 XTP3, Ireland (email: info@hbgi.ie)

Distributed in the US by Hachette Book Group
1290 Avenue of the Americas, 4th and 5th Floors
New York, NY 10104

Distributed in Canada by Canadian Manda Group
664 Annette St., Toronto, Ontario, Canada M6S 2C8

ISBN 978-1-7884-0683-3
eISBN 978-1-7884-0728-1

A CIP catalogue record for this book is available from the British Library.

Printed and bound in Great Britain.

10 9 8 7 6 5 4 3 2 1

Publisher: Lucy Pessell
Senior Designer: Alicia House
Senior Editor: Katie Button
Assistant Editor: Samina Rahman
Production Manager: Allison Gonsalves

Picture Credits: iStock/Extezty, ggodby

FSC www.fsc.org
MIX
Paper | Supporting responsible forestry
FSC® C104740

This FSC® label means that materials used for the product have been responsibly sourced.

MERMAIDS SIRENS & CREATURES OF THE WATERS

AN ANTHOLOGY OF CLASSIC POETRY & STORIES

AURORA THORNE

GODSFIELD

CONTENTS

INTRODUCTION

Throughout history, we have been drawn to the water: oceans, lakes and rivers have been a source of inspiration, mystery and danger. Poets and artists have heard and responded to the siren call of the deep and the fascinating creatures – including mermaids, sirens, nixies and nymphs – that live there. The tales and poems in this collection are a journey into the world of mermaids, sirens and other creatures of the water, and the mythologies from which they arose. They invite and encourage reflection on our own relationship with the mysteries of the ocean. The creatures in these pages do not solely inhabit the darkest nadirs of the sea, but also the enormous depths of our imagination. They occupy a space that delicately balances the beauty, mystery and fear of setting out into unknown waters.

Mermaids and water fairies are sometimes beautiful and may play with and tease adventurers and romantics. They are often described as having long hair and a beautiful face, and are known as great singers, drawing sailors from their ships with their ethereal voices. While many depictions of mermaids signify freedom, grace and the unrestrained allure of deep waters, they also symbolize the most dangerous aspects – death, destruction and tragedy. It is this combination of mythical beauty and a sense of danger that explains the power of these creatures across many literary works. They offer the seduction of the world beneath the waves, but warn of the perils that lie waiting within. Stories and poems of love, loss and longing, each tale draws on the universal themes of desire, fear and belonging that speak to the all-too-human experience of desire and unrequited love in all its complexity.

The siren is a darker sister to the mermaid, evolved into a dangerous personification of temptation gone wrong. Sirens were often depicted as evil creatures who lured sailors to the sea with their enchanting songs before killing them. They tell us that not everything that glitters in the ocean has our best interest at heart. The song of the sirens is lovely enough to attract our attention, yet destructive enough to steal our souls – the chorus warning us that the price of desire is high.

The narratives of selkies, kelpies, Lorelei, Rhinemaidens and any number of mythical water creatures are woven through societies across time and geography, reflecting and shaping the anxieties and fascinations of the cultures in which they appeared. Through these classic stories and poems, we embrace the timeless exploration of unknown waters, a dance between humanity and the deep ocean, where every tale adds depth to our understanding.

SIRENS

We have heard the mer-maidens singing, and know that we shall never see dry land any more
— Robert Louis Stevenson

THE STORY OF THE SIREN

E M FORSTER

Few things have been more beautiful than my note book on the Deist Controversy as it fell downward through the waters of the Mediterranean. It dived, like a piece of black slate, but opened soon, disclosing leaves of pale green, which quivered into blue. Now it had vanished, now it was a piece of magical India rubber stretching out to infinity, now it was a book again, but bigger than the book of all knowledge. It grew more fantastic as it reached the bottom, where a puff of sand welcomed it and obscured it from view. But it reappeared, quite sane though a little tremulous, lying decently open on its back, while unseen fingers fidgeted among its leaves.

'It is such a pity' said my aunt, 'that you will not finish your work in the Hotel. Then you would be free to enjoy yourself and this would never have happened.'

'Nothing of it but will change into something rich and strange,' warbled the chaplain, while his sister said 'Why it's gone into the water.' As for the boatmen, one of them laughed, while the other, without a word of warning, stood up and began to take his clothes off.

'Holy Moses!' cried the Colonel. 'Is the fellow mad?'

'Yes, thank him dear,' said my aunt: 'that is to say tell him he is very kind, but perhaps another time.'

'All the same I do want my book back,' I complained. 'It's for my Fellowship Dissertation. There won't be much left of it by another time.'

'I have an idea,' said some woman or other through her parasol. 'Let us leave this child of nature to dive for the book while we go on to the other grotto. We can land him either on this rock or on the ledge inside, and he will be ready when we return.'

The idea seemed good; and I improved it by saying I would be left behind too, to lighten the boat. So the two of us were deposited outside the little grotto on a great sunlit rock that guarded the harmonies within. Let us call them blue, though they suggest rather the spirit of what is clean, cleanliness passed from the domestic to the sublime, the cleanliness of all the sea gathered together and radiating light. The Blue Grotto at Capri contains only more blue water, not bluer water. That colour and that spirit is the heritage of every cave in the Mediterranean into which the sun can shine and the sea flow.

As soon as the boat left I realised how imprudent I had been to trust myself on a sloping rock with an unknown Sicilian. With a jerk he became alive, seizing my arm and saying 'Go to the end of the Grotto and I will show you something beautiful.'

He made me jump off the rock on to the ledge over a dazzling crack of sea, he drew me away from the light till I was standing on the tiny beach of sand which emerged like powdered turquoise at the further end. There he left me with his clothes, and returned swiftly to the summit of the entrance-rock. For a moment he stood naked in the brilliant sun, looking down at the spot where the book lay. Then he crossed himself, raised his hands above his head, and dived. If the book was wonderful, the man is past all description. His effect was that of a silver statue, alive beneath the sea, through whom life throbbed in blue and green. Something infinitely happy, infinitely wise – but it was impossible that it should emerge from the depths sunburnt and dripping, holding the note book on the Deist Controversy between its teeth.

A gratuity is generally expected by those who bathe. Whatever I offered, he was sure to want more, and I was disinclined for an argument in a place so beautiful and also so solitary. It was a relief that he should say in conversational tones 'In a place like this one might see the Siren.'

I was delighted with him for thus falling into the key of his surroundings. We had been left together in a magic world, apart from all the commonplaces that are called reality, a world of blue whose floor was the sea and whose walls and roof of rock trembled with the sea's reflections. Here, only the fantastic would be tolerable, and it was in that spirit that I echoed his words. 'One might easily see the Siren.'

He watched me curiously while he dressed. I was parting the sticky leaves of the note book as I sat on the strip of sand.

'Ah!' he said at last. 'You may have read the little book that was printed last year. Who would have thought that our Siren would have given the foreigners pleasure!'

(I read it afterwards. Its account is, not unnaturally, incomplete, in spite of there being a woodcut of the young person, and the words of her song.)

'She comes out of this blue water, doesn't she,' I suggested 'and sits on the rock at the entrance, combing her hair.'

I wanted to draw him out, for I was interested in his sudden gravity, and there was a suggestion of irony in his last remark that puzzled me.

'Have you ever seen her?'

'Often and often.'

'I never.'

'But you have heard her sing!'

He put on his coat and said impatiently, 'How can she sing under the water? Who could? She sometimes tries, but nothing comes from her but great bubbles.'

'She should climb on to the rock then.'

'How can she?' he cried again, quite angry. 'The priests have blessed the air, so she cannot breathe it, and blessed the rocks, so that she cannot sit on them. But the sea no man can bless, because it is too big, and always changing. Therefore she lives in the sea.'

I was silent.

At this his face took a gentler expression. He looked at me as though something was on his mind, and going out to the entrance rock, gazed at the external blue. Then returning into our twilight he said 'As a rule only good people see the Siren.'

I made no comment. There was a pause, and he continued. 'That is a very strange thing, and the priests do not know how to account for it; for she of course is wicked. Not only those who fast and go to mass are in danger, but even those who are merely good in daily life. No one in the village had seen her for two generations. I am not surprised. We all cross ourselves before we enter the water, but it is unnecessary. Giuseppe, we thought, was safer than most. We loved him, and many of us he loved: but that is a different thing to being good.'

I asked who Giuseppe was.

'That day – I was seventeen and my brother was twenty and a great deal stronger than I was and it was the year when the visitors, who have brought such prosperity and so many alterations into the village, first began to come. One English lady in particular, of very high birth, came, and has written a book about the place, and it was through her that the Improvement Syndicate was formed, which is about to connect the hotels with the station by means of a Funicular railway.'

'Don't tell me about that lady in here,' I observed.

'That day we took her and her friends to see the grottoes.

As we rowed close under the cliffs I put out my hand, as one does, and caught a little crab, and having pulled off its claws offered it as a curiosity. The ladies groaned, but a gentleman was pleased, and held out money. Being inexperienced, I refused it, saying that his pleasure was sufficient reward! Giuseppe, who was rowing behind, was very angry with me and reached out with his hand and hit me on the side of the mouth, so that a tooth cut my lip, and I bled. I tried to hit him back, but he always was too quick for me, and as I stretched round he kicked me under the arm pit, so that for a moment I could not even row. There was a great noise among the ladies, and I heard afterwards that they were planning to take me away from my brother and train me as a waiter. That at all events never came to pass.

'When we reached the grotto – not here, but a larger one – the gentleman was very anxious that one of us should dive for money, and the ladies consented, as they sometimes do. Giuseppe who had discovered how much pleasure it gives foreigners to see us in the water, refused to dive for anything but silver, and the gentleman threw in a two lira piece.

'Just before my brother sprang off he caught sight of me holding my bruise, and crying, for I could not help it. He laughed and said "this time, at all events, I shall not see the Siren!" and went into the blue water without crossing himself. But he saw her.'

He broke off, and accepted a cigarette. I watched the golden entrance rock and the quivering walls, and the magic water through which great bubbles constantly rose. At last he dropped his hot ash into the ripples and turned his head away, and said:

'He came up without the coin. We pulled him into the boat, and he was so large that he seemed to fill it, and so wet that we could not dress him. I have never seen a man so wet. I and the gentleman rowed back, and we covered Giuseppe with sacking and propped him up in the stern.'

'He was drowned, then?' I murmured, supposing that to be the point.

'He was not' he cried angrily. 'He saw the Siren. I told you.'

I was silenced again.

'We put him to bed, though he was not ill. The doctor came, and took money, and the priest came and took more and smothered him with incense and spattered him with holy water. But it was no good. He was too big—like a piece of the sea. He kissed the thumb-bones of San Biagio and they never dried till evening.'

'What did he look like?' I ventured.

'Like anyone who has seen the Siren. If you have seen her "often and often" how is it you do not know? Unhappy, unhappy, unhappy because he knew everything. Every living thing made him unhappy because he knew it would die. And all he cared to do was to sleep.'

I bent over my note book.

'He did no work, he forgot to eat, he forgot whether he had his clothes on. All the work fell on me, and my sister had to go out to service. We tried to make him into a beggar, but he was too robust to inspire pity, and as for an idiot, he had not the right look in his eyes. He would stand in the street looking at people, and the more he looked at them the more unhappy he became. When a child was born he would cover his face with his hands. If anyone was married – he was terrible then, and would frighten them as they came out of church. Who would have believed he would marry himself! I caused that, I. I was reading out of the paper how a girl at Ragusa had "gone mad through bathing in the sea." Giuseppe got up, and in a week he and that girl came in together.

'He never told me anything, but it seems that he went straight to her house, broke into her room, and carried her off. She was the daughter of a rich mine-owner, so you may imagine our peril. Her father came down, with a clever lawyer, but they could do no more than I. They argued and they threatened, but at last they had to go back and we lost nothing – that is to say, no money. We took Giuseppe and Maria to the Church and had them married. Ugh! that wedding! The priest made no jokes afterwards and coming out the children threw stones... I think I would have died to make her happy; but as always happens, one could do nothing.'

'Were they unhappy together then?'

'They loved each other, but love is not happiness. We can all get love. Love is nothing. Love is everywhere since the death of Jesus Christ. I had two people to work for now, for she was like him in everything – one never knew which of them was speaking. I had to sell our own boat and work under the bad old man you have to-day. Worst of all, people began to hate us. The children first – everything begins with them – and then the women and last of all the men. For the cause of every misfortune was – you will not betray me?'

I promised good faith, and immediately he burst into the frantic blasphemy of one who has escaped from supervision, cursing the priests, the lying filthy cheating immoral priests who had ruined his life, who had murdered his brother and the girl, whom he dared not murder back because they held the key of heaven and could ruin him in the next life too. 'Thus are we tricked!' was his cry and he stood up and kicked at the azure ripples with his feet, till he had obscured them with a cloud of sand.

I too was moved. The story of Giuseppe, for all its absurdity and superstition, came nearer to reality than anything I had known before. I don't know why, but it filled me with desire to help others – the greatest of all our desires I suppose, and the most fruitless. The desire soon passed.

'She was about to have a child. That was the end of everything. People said to me 'When will your charming nephew be born? What a cheerful attractive child he will be, with such a father and mother!' I kept my face steady and replied 'I think he may be. Out of sadness shall come gladness' – it is one of our proverbs. And my answer frightened them very much, and they told the priests, who were frightened too. Then the whisper started that the child would be Anti-Christ: you need not be afraid: he was never born.

'An old witch began to prophesy, and no one stopped her. Giuseppe and the girl, she said, had silent devils, who could do little harm. But the child would always be speaking and laughing and perverting, and last of all he would go into the sea and fetch up the Siren into the air and all the world would see her and hear her sing. As soon as she sang, the Seven Vials would be opened and the Pope would die and Mongibello flame, and the veil of Santa Agata would be burnt. Then the boy and the Siren would marry, and together they would rule the world, for ever and ever.

'The whole village was in tumult, and the hotel keepers became alarmed, for the tourist season was just beginning. They met together and decided that Giuseppe and the girl must be sent inland until the child was born, and they subscribed the money. The night before they were to start there was a full moon and wind from the east, and all along the coast the sea shot up over the cliffs in silver clouds. It is a wonderful sight, and Maria said she must see it once more.

'"Do not go," I said. "I saw the priest go by, and someone with him. And the hotel keepers do not like you to be seen, and if we displease them also we shall starve."

'"I want to go," she replied. "The sea is stormy, and I may never feel it again."

'"No, he is right" said Giuseppe. "Do not go – or let one of us go with you."

'"I want to go alone," she said; and she went alone.

'I tied up their luggage in a piece of cloth, and then I was so unhappy at thinking I should lose them that I went and sat down by my brother and put my arm round his neck, and he put his arm round me, which he had not done for more than a year, and we remained thus I don't remember how long.

'Suddenly the door flew open and moon-light and wind came in together, and a child's voice said laughing "They have pushed her over the cliffs into the sea."

'I stepped to the drawer where I keep my knives, and the child ran away.

"Sit down again" said Giuseppe – Giuseppe of all people! "If she is dead, why should others die too?"

"I guess who it is," I cried, "and I will kill him."

'I was almost out of the door but he tripped me up and kneeling upon me took hold of both my hands and sprained my wrists; first my right one, then my left. No one but Giuseppe would have thought of such a thing. It hurt more than you would suppose, and I fainted. When I woke up, he was gone, and I have never seen him again.'

But Giuseppe disgusted me.

'I told you he was wicked,' he said. 'No one would have expected him to see the Siren.'

'How do you know he did see her then?'

'Because he did not see her "often and often" but once.'

'Why do you love him if he is wicked?'

He laughed for the first time. That was his only reply.

'Is that the end?' I asked, feeling curiously ashamed.

'I never killed her murderer, for by the time my wrists were well, he was in America; and one cannot kill a priest. As for Giuseppe, he went all over the world too, looking for someone else who has seen the Siren – either a man, or, better still, a woman, for then the child might still have been born. At last he came to Liverpool, – is the district probable? – and there he began to cough, and spat blood until he died.

'I do not suppose there is anyone living now who has seen her. There has seldom been more than one in a generation, and never in my life will there be both a man and a woman from whom that child can be born, who will fetch up the Siren from the sea, and destroy silence, and save the world!'

'Save the world?' I cried. 'Did the prophecy end like that?'

He leant back against the rock, breathing deep. Through all the blue-green reflections I saw him colour. I heard him say: 'Silence and loneliness cannot last for ever. It may be a hundred or a thousand years, but the sea lasts longer, and she shall come out of it and sing.' I would have asked him more, but at that moment the whole cave darkened, and there rode in through its narrow entrance the returning boat.

SONNET 119

WILLIAM SHAKESPEARE

What potions have I drunk of Siren tears,
Distill'd from limbecks foul as hell within,
Applying fears to hopes and hopes to fears,
Still losing when I saw myself to win!
What wretched errors hath my heart committed,
Whilst it hath thought itself so blessed never!
How have mine eyes out of their spheres been fitted
In the distraction of this madding fever!
O benefit of ill! now I find true
That better is by evil still made better;
And ruin'd love, when it is built anew,
Grows fairer than at first, more strong, far greater.
So I return rebuk'd to my content,
And gain by ill thrice more than I have spent.

from
THE MERMAID

ANNE BANNERMAN

Eternal world of waters, hail!
Within thy caves my Lover lies;
And day and night alike shall fail
Ere slumber lock my streaming eyes.
Along this wild untrodden coast,
Heap'd by the gelid' hand of frost;
Thro' this unbounded waste of seas,
Where never sigh'd the vernal breeze;
Mine was the choice, in this terrific form,
To brave the icy surge, to shiver in the storm.

Yes! I am chang'd – My heart, my soul,
Retain no more their former glow.
Hence, ere the black'ning tempests roll,
I watch the bark, in murmurs low,
(While darker low'rs the thick'ning' gloom)
To lure the sailor to his doom;
Soft from some pile of frozen snow
I pour the syren-song of woe;
Like the sad mariner's expiring cry,
As, faint and worn with toil, he lays him down to die.

Then, while the dark and angry deep
Hangs his huge billows high in air ;
And the wild wind with awful sweep,
Howls in each fitful swell – beware!
Firm on the rent and crashing mast,
I lend new fury to the blast;
I mark each hardy cheek grow pale,

And the proud sons of courage fail;
Till the torn vessel drinks the surging waves,
Yawns the disparted main, and opes its shelving graves.

When Vengeance bears along the wave
The spell, which heav'n and earth appals;
Alone, by night, in darksome cave,
On me the gifted wizard calls.
Above the ocean's boiling flood
Thro' vapour glares the moon in blood:
Low sounds along the waters die,
And shrieks of anguish fill the' sky;
Convulsive powers the solid rocks divide,
While, o'er the heaving surge, the embodied spirits glide.

Thrice welcome to my weary sight,
Avenging ministers of Wrath!
Ye heard, amid the realms of night,
The spell that wakes the sleep of death.
Where Hecla's flames the snows dissolve,
Or storms, the polar skies involve;
Where, o'er the tempest-beaten wreck,
The raging winds and billows break;
On the sad earth, and in the stormy sea,
All, all shall shudd'ring own your potent agency.

To aid your toils, to scatter death,
Swift, as the sheeted lightning's force,
When the keen north-wind's freezing breath
Spreads desolation in its course,
My soul within this icy sea,
Fulfils her fearful destiny.
Thro' Time's long ages I shall wait
To lead the victims to their fate;
With callous heart, to hidden rocks decoy,
And lure, in seraph-strains, unpitying, to destroy.

ISLE OF MAN

WILLIAM WORDSWORTH

A youth too certain of his power to wade
On the smooth bottom of this clear bright sea,
To sight so shallow, with a bather's glee,
Leapt from this rock, and but for timely aid
He, by the alluring element betrayed,
Had perished. Then might Sea-nymphs (and with sighs
Of self-reproach) have chanted elegies
Bewailing his sad fate, when he was laid
In peaceful earth: for, doubtless, he was frank,
Utterly in himself devoid of guile;
Knew not the double-dealing of a smile;
Nor aught that makes men's promises a blank,
Or deadly snare: and He survives to bless
The Power that saved him in his strange distress.

THE SIRENS' SONG

WILLIAM BROWNE

Steer, hither steer your wingèd pines,
All beaten mariners!
Here lie Love's undiscover'd mines,
A prey to passengers–
Perfumes far sweeter than the best
Which make the Phoenix' urn and nest.
Fear not your ships,
Nor any to oppose you save our lips;
But come on shore,
Where no joy dies till Love hath gotten more.

For swelling waves our panting breasts,
Where never storms arise,
Exchange, and be awhile our guests:
For stars gaze on our eyes.
The compass Love shall hourly sing,
And as he goes about the ring,
We will not miss
To tell each point he nameth with a kiss.
–Then come on shore,
Where no joy dies till Love hath gotten more.

THE SEA-FAIRIES

ALFRED, LORD TENNYSON

Slow sail'd the weary mariners and saw,
Betwixt the green brink and the running foam,
Sweet faces, rounded arms, and bosoms prest
To little harps of gold; and while they mused
Whispering to each other half in fear,
Shrill music reach'd them on the middle sea.

Whither away, whither away, whither away? fly no more.
Whither away from the high green field,
and the happy blossoming shore?
Day and night to the billow the fountain calls:
Down shower the gambolling waterfalls
From wandering over the lea;
Out of the live-green heart of the dells
They freshen the silvery-crimson shells,
And thick with white bells the clover-hill swells
High over the full-toned sea:
O hither, come hither and furl your sails,
Come hither to me and to me:
Hither, come hither and frolic and play;
Here it is only the mew that wails;
We will sing to you all the day:

Mariner, mariner, furl your sails,
For here are the blissful downs and dales,
And merrily, merrily carol the gales
And the spangle dances in bight and bay,
And the rainbow forms and flies on the land
Over the islands free;
And the rainbow lives in the curve of the sand;
Hither, come hither and see;
And the rainbow hangs on the poising wave,
And sweet is the colour of cove and cave,
And sweet shall your welcome be:
Oh hither, come hither, and be our lords,
For merry brides are we:
We will kiss sweet kisses, and speak sweet words.
Oh listen, listen, your eyes shall glisten
With pleasure and love and jubilee:
Oh listen, listen, your eyes shall glisten,
When the sharp clear twang of the golden chords
Runs up the ridged sea.
Who can light on as happy a shore
All the world o'er, all the world o'er
Whither away? listen and stay:
mariner, mariner, fly no more.

A SEA-SPELL

DANTE GABRIEL ROSSETTI

Her lute hangs shadowed in the apple-tree,
While flashing fingers weave the sweet-strung spell
Between its chords; and as the wild notes swell,
The sea-bird for those branches leaves the sea.
But to what sound her listening ear stoops she?
What netherworld gulf-whispers doth she hear?
In answering echoes from what planisphere,
Along the wind, along the estuary?

She sinks into her spell: and when full soon
Her lips move and she soars
into her song,
What creatures of the midmost main shall throng
In furrowed surf-clouds to the summoning rune:
Till he, the fated mariner, hears her cry,
And up her rock, bare-breasted, comes to die?

from THE DIVINE COMEDY

DANTE ALIGHIERI

There came to me in dreams a stammering woman,
Squint in her eyes, and in her feet distorted,
With hands dissevered and of sallow hue.

I looked at her; and as the sun restores
The frigid members which the night benumbs,
Even thus my gaze did render voluble

Her tongue, and made her all erect thereafter
In little while, and the lost countenance
As love desires it so in her did colour.

When in this wise she had her speech unloosed,
She 'gan to sing so, that with difficulty
Could I have turned my thoughts away from her.

'I am,' she sang, 'I am the Siren sweet
Who mariners amid the main unman,
So full am I of pleasantness to hear.

I drew Ulysses from his wandering way
Unto my song, and he who dwells with me
Seldom departs so wholly I content him.'

THE SIRENS

JAMES RUSSELL LOWELL

The sea is lonely, the sea is dreary,
The sea is restless and uneasy;
Thou seekest quiet, thou art weary,
Wandering thou knowest not whither;–
Our little isle is green and breezy,
Come and rest thee! Oh come hither,
Come to this peaceful home of ours,
Where evermore
The low west-wind creeps panting up the shore
To be at rest among the flowers;
Full of rest, the green moss lifts,
As the dark waves of the sea
Draw in and out of rocky rifts,
Calling solemnly to thee
With voices deep and hollow,–
'To the shore
Follow! Oh, follow!
To be at rest forevermore!
Forevermore!'

Look how the gray old Ocean
From the depth of his heart rejoices,
Heaving with a gentle motion,
When he hears our restful voices;
List how he sings in an undertone,
Chiming with our melody;
And all sweet sounds of earth and air
Melt into one low voice alone,
That murmurs over the weary sea,
And seems to sing from everywhere,–

'Here mayst thou harbor peacefully,
Here mayst thou rest from the aching oar;
Turn thy curvëd prow ashore,
And in our green isle rest forevermore!
Forevermore!'
And Echo half wakes in the wooded hill,
And, to her heart so calm and deep,
Murmurs over in her sleep,
Doubtfully pausing and murmuring still,
'Evermore!'
Thus, on Life's weary sea,
Heareth the marinere
Voices sweet, from far and near,
Ever singing low and clear,
Ever singing longingly.

It is not better here to be,
Than to be toiling late and soon?
In the dreary night to see
Nothing but the blood-red moon
Go up and down into the sea;
Or, in the loneliness of day,
To see the still seals only
Solemnly lift their faces gray,
Making it yet more lonely?
Is it not better than to hear
Only the sliding of the wave
Beneath the plank, and feel so near
A cold and lonely grave,
A restless grave, where thou shalt lie

Even in death unquietly?
Look down beneath thy wave-worn bark,
Lean over the side and see
The leaden eye of the sidelong shark
Upturnëd patiently,
Ever waiting there for thee:
Look down and see those shapeless forms,
Which ever keep their dreamless sleep
Far down within the gloomy deep,
And only stir themselves in storms,
Rising like islands from beneath,
And snorting through the angry spray,
As the frail vessel perisheth
In the whirls of their unwieldy play;
Look down! Look down!
Upon the seaweed, slimy and dark,
That waves its arms so lank and brown,
Beckoning for thee!
Look down beneath thy wave-worn bark
Into the cold depth of the sea!
Look down! Look down!
Thus, on Life's lonely sea,
Heareth the marinere
Voices sad, from far and near,
Ever singing full of fear,
Ever singing dreadfully.

Here all is pleasant as a dream;
The wind scarce shaketh down the dew,
The green grass floweth like a stream
Into the ocean's blue;
Listen! Oh, listen!
Here is a gush of many streams,
A song of many birds,
And every wish and longing seems

Lulled to a numbered flow of words,–
Listen! Oh, listen!
Here ever hum the golden bees
Underneath full-blossomed trees,
At once with glowing fruit and flowers crowned;–
So smooth the sand, the yellow sand,
That thy keel will not grate as it touches the land;
All around with a slumberous sound,
The singing waves slide up the strand,
And there, where the smooth, wet pebbles be
The waters gurgle longingly,
As if they fain would seek the shore,
To be at rest from the ceaseless roar,
To be at rest forevermore,–
Forevermore.

Thus, on Life's gloomy sea,
Heareth the marinere
Voices sweet, from far and near,
Ever singing in his ear,
'Here is rest and peace for thee!'

THE SONG OF THE SIREN

MARIETTA HOLLEY

Oh, I am the siren, the siren of the sea,
The sea, the wondrous sea, that lies forevermore before;
I stand a fairy shape upon the shadow of a cliff
Where the water's drowsy ripple laps the phantom of a shore,
And, oh, so fair, so fair am I, I draw all hearts to me,
For I am the siren, the siren of the sea.

All the glory of my golden tresses gleams upon the air,
How it falls about my snowy shoulders,
round and bare and white;
My lips are full of love as rounded grapes are full of wine,
And my eyes are large and languid, and full of dewy light;
Oh, I lure the idle landsmen many a league for love of me,
For I am the siren, the siren of the sea.

Sometimes they press so near that my breath is on their cheek,
And their eager hands can almost touch the
glowing bowl I bear,
They can see the beaded froth, the ruby glitter of the wine,
Then I slip from their embraces like a breath of summer air;
Oh, I lightly, lightly glide away, they come no nigher me,
For I am the siren, the siren of the sea.

Sometimes I float along a-standing in a boat,
Before the ships becalmed, where dusky sailors stand,
And the helmsman drops his oar, and the lookout
leaves his glass,
So I beckon them, and lure them, with the whiteness
of my hand;
Oh, this the song I sing, well they listen unto me?
For I am the siren, the siren of the sea.

Would you from toil and labor flee,
Oh float ye out on this wonderful sea,
From islands of spice the zephyrs blow,
Swaying the galleys to and fro;
Silken sails and a balmy breeze
Shall waft you unto a perfect ease.

Fold your hands and rest, and rest,
The sun sails on from the east to the west,
The days will come, and the days will go,
What good can man for his labor show
In passionless peace, come float with me
Over the waves of this wonderful sea.

Would you forget, oh sorrowful soul,
Come and drink of this golden bowl,
With jewelled poppies about the rim,
Drink of the wine that flushes its brim,
And drown all your haunting memories there,
Your woe and your weary care.

Oh, I am the siren, the siren of the sea,
The sea, the wondrous sea, that lies forevermore before;
Oh, the mystic music ripples, how they break in rosy spray,
But the crystal wave will mock them, they will
reach it nevermore,
For it glides away, I glide away, they come no nigher me,
For I am the siren, the siren of the sea.

from
THE COMEDY OF ERRORS

WILLIAM SHAKESPEARE

O, train me not, sweet mermaid, with thy note,
To drown me in thy sister's flood of tears:
Sing, siren, for thyself and I will dote:
Spread o'er the silver waves thy golden hairs,
And as a bed I'll take them and there lie,
And in that glorious supposition think
He gains by death that hath such means to die:
Let Love, being light, be drowned if she sink!

from THE ODYSSEY

HOMER

After we were clear of the river Oceanus, and had got out into the open sea, we went on till we reached the Aeaean island where there is dawn and sun-rise as in other places. We then drew our ship on to the sands and got out of her on to the shore, where we went to sleep and waited till day should break.

Then, when the child of morning, rosy-fingered Dawn, appeared, I sent some men to Circe's house to fetch the body of Elpenor. We cut firewood from a wood where the headland jutted out into the sea, and after we had wept over him and lamented him we performed his funeral rites. When his body and armour had been burned to ashes, we raised a cairn, set a stone over it, and at the top of the cairn we fixed the oar that he had been used to row with.

While we were doing all this, Circe, who knew that we had got back from the house of Hades, dressed herself and came to us as fast as she could; and her maid servants came with her bringing us bread, meat, and wine. Then she stood in the midst of us and said, 'You have done a bold thing in going down alive to the house of Hades, and you will have died twice, to other people's once; now, then, stay here for the rest of the day, feast your fill, and go on with your voyage at daybreak tomorrow morning. In the meantime I will tell Ulysses about your course, and will explain everything to him so as to prevent your suffering from misadventure either by land or sea.'

We agreed to do as she had said, and feasted through the livelong day to the going down of the sun, but when the sun had set and it came on dark, the men laid themselves down to sleep by the stern cables of the ship. Then Circe took me by the hand and bade me be seated away from the others, while she reclined by my side and asked me all about our adventures.

'So far so good,' said she, when I had ended my story, 'and now pay attention to what I am about to tell you – heaven itself, indeed, will recall it to your recollection. First you will come to the Sirens who enchant all who come near them. If any one unwarily draws in too close and hears the singing of the Sirens, his wife and children will never welcome him home again, for they sit in a green field and warble him to death with the sweetness of their song. There is a great heap of dead men's bones lying all around, with the flesh still rotting off them. Therefore pass these Sirens by, and stop your men's ears with wax that none of them may hear; but if you like you can listen yourself, for you may get the men to bind you as you stand upright on a cross piece half way up the mast, and they must lash the rope's ends to the mast itself, that you may have the pleasure of listening. If you beg and pray the men to unloose you, then they must bind you faster.

'When your crew have taken you past these Sirens, I cannot give you coherent directions as to which of two courses you are to take; I will lay the two alternatives before you, and you must consider them for yourself. On the one hand there are some overhanging rocks against which the deep blue waves of Amphitrite beat with terrific fury; the blessed gods call these rocks the Wanderers. Here not even a bird may pass, no, not even the timid doves that bring ambrosia to Father Jove, but the sheer rock always carries off one of them, and Father Jove has to send another to make up their number; no ship that ever yet came to these rocks has got away again, but the waves and whirlwinds of fire are freighted with wreckage and with the bodies of dead men. The only vessel that ever sailed and got through, was the famous Argo on her way from the house of Aetes, and she too would have gone against these great rocks, only that Juno piloted her past them for the love she bore to Jason.

'Of these two rocks the one reaches heaven and its peak is lost in a dark cloud. This never leaves it, so that the top is never clear not even in summer and early autumn. No man though he had twenty hands and twenty feet could get a foothold on it and climb it, for it runs sheer up, as smooth as though it had been polished. In the middle of it there is a large cavern, looking West and turned towards Erebus; you must take your ship this way, but the cave is so high up that not even the stoutest archer could send an arrow into it. Inside it Scylla sits and yelps with a voice that you might take to be that of a young hound, but in truth she is a dreadful monster and no one – not even a god – could face her without being terror-struck. She has twelve mis-shapen feet, and six necks of the most prodigious length; and at the end of each neck she has a frightful head with three rows of teeth in each, all set very close together, so that they would crunch any one to death in a moment, and she sits deep within her shady cell thrusting out her heads and peering all round the rock, fishing for dolphins or dogfish or any larger monster that she can catch, of the thousands with which Amphitrite teems. No ship ever yet got past her without losing some men, for she shoots out all her heads at once, and carries off a man in each mouth.

'You will find the other rock lie lower, but they are so close together that there is not more than a bow-shot between them. A large fig tree in full leaf grows upon it, and under it lies the sucking whirlpool of Charybdis. Three times in the day does she vomit forth her waters, and three times she sucks them down again; see that you be not there when she is sucking, for if you are, Neptune himself could not save you; you must hug the Scylla side and drive ship by as fast as you can, for you had better lose six men than your whole crew.'

'Is there no way,' said I, 'of escaping Charybdis, and at the same time keeping Scylla off when she is trying to harm my men?'

'You dare devil,' replied the goddess, 'you are always wanting to fight somebody or something; you will not let yourself be beaten even by the immortals. For Scylla is not mortal; moreover she is savage, extreme, rude, cruel and invincible. There is no help for it; your best chance will be to get by her as fast as ever you can, for if you dawdle about her rock while you are putting on your armour, she may catch you with a second cast of her six heads, and snap up another half dozen of your men; so drive your ship past her at full speed, and roar out lustily to Crataiis who is Scylla's dam, bad luck to her; she will then stop her from making a second raid upon you.'

'You will now come to the Thrinacian island, and here you will see many herds of cattle and flocks of sheep belonging to the sun-god – seven herds of cattle and seven flocks of sheep, with fifty head in each flock. They do not breed, nor do they become fewer in number, and they are tended by the goddesses Phaethusa and Lampetie, who are children of the sun-god Hyperion by Neaera. Their mother when she had borne them and had done suckling them sent them to the Thrinacian island, which was a long way off, to live there and look after their father's flocks and herds. If you leave these flocks unharmed, and think of nothing but getting home, you may yet after much hardship reach Ithaca; but if you harm them, then I forewarn you of the destruction both of your ship and of your comrades; and even though you may yourself escape, you will return late, in bad plight, after losing all your men.'

Here she ended, and dawn enthroned in gold began to show in heaven, whereon she returned inland. I then went on board and told my men to loose the ship from her moorings; so they at once got into her, took their places, and began to smite the grey sea with their oars. Presently the great and cunning goddess Circe befriended us with a fair wind that blew dead aft, and staid steadily with us, keeping our sails well filled, so we did whatever wanted doing to the ship's gear, and let her go as wind and helmsman headed her.

Then, being much troubled in mind, I said to my men, 'My friends, it is not right that one or two of us alone should know the prophecies that Circe has made me, I will therefore tell you about them, so that whether we live or die we may do so with our eyes open. First she said we were to keep clear of the Sirens, who sit and sing most beautifully in a field of flowers; but she said I might hear them myself so long as no one else did. Therefore, take me and bind me to the crosspiece half way up the mast; bind me as I stand upright, with a bond so fast that I cannot possibly break away, and lash the rope's ends to the mast itself. If I beg and pray you to set me free, then bind me more tightly still.'

I had hardly finished telling everything to the men before we reached the island of the two Sirens, for the wind had been very favourable. Then all of a sudden it fell dead calm; there was not a breath of wind nor a ripple upon the water, so the men furled the sails and stowed them; then taking to their oars they whitened the water with the foam they raised in rowing. Meanwhile I look a large wheel of wax and cut it up small with my sword. Then I kneaded the wax in my strong hands till it became soft, which it soon did between the kneading and the rays of the sun-god son of Hyperion. Then I stopped the ears of all my men, and they bound me hands and feet to the mast as I stood upright on the cross piece; but they went on rowing themselves. When we had got within earshot of the land, and the ship was going at a good rate, the Sirens saw that we were getting in shore and began with their singing.

'Come here,' they sang, 'renowned Ulysses, honour to the Achaean name, and listen to our two voices. No one ever sailed past us without staying to hear the enchanting sweetness of our song – and he who listens will go on his way not only charmed, but wiser, for we know all the ills that the gods laid upon the Argives and Trojans before Troy, and can tell you everything that is going to happen over the whole world.'

They sang these words most musically, and as I longed to hear them further I made signs by frowning to my men that they should set me free; but they quickened their stroke, and Eurylochus and Perimedes bound me with still stronger bonds till we had got out of hearing of the Sirens' voices. Then my men took the wax from their ears and unbound me.

Immediately after we had got past the island I saw a great wave from which spray was rising, and I heard a loud roaring sound. The men were so frightened that they loosed hold of their oars, for the whole sea resounded with the rushing of the waters, but the ship stayed where it was, for the men had left off rowing. I went round, therefore, and exhorted them man by man not to lose heart.

'My friends,' said I, 'this is not the first time that we have been in danger, and we are in nothing like so bad a case as when the Cyclops shut us up in his cave; nevertheless, my courage and wise counsel saved us then, and we shall live to look back on all this as well. Now, therefore, let us all do as I say, trust in Jove and row on with might and main. As for you, coxswain, these are your orders; attend to them, for the ship is in your hands; turn her head away from these steaming rapids and hug the rock, or she will give you the slip and be over yonder before you know where you are, and you will be the death of us.'

So they did as I told them; but I said nothing about the awful monster Scylla, for I knew the men would not go on rowing if I did, but would huddle together in the hold. In one thing only did I disobey Circe's strict instructions – I put on my armour. Then seizing two strong spears I took my stand on the ship's bows, for it was there that I expected first to see the monster of the rock, who was to do my men so much harm; but I could not make her out anywhere, though I strained my eyes with looking the gloomy rock all over and over.

Then we entered the Straits in great fear of mind, for on the one hand was Scylla, and on the other dread Charybdis kept sucking up the salt water. As she vomited it up, it was like the water in a cauldron when it is boiling over upon a great fire, and the spray reached the top of the rocks on either side. When she began to suck again, we could see the water all inside whirling round and round, and it made a deafening sound as it broke against the rocks. We could see the bottom of the whirlpool all black with sand and mud, and the men were at their wits ends for fear. While we were taken up with this, and were expecting each moment to be our last, Scylla pounced down suddenly upon us and snatched up my six best men. I was looking at once after both ship and men, and in a moment I saw their hands and feet ever so high above me, struggling in the air as Scylla was carrying them off, and I heard them call out my name in one last despairing cry. As a fisherman, seated, spear in hand, upon some jutting rock throws bait into the water to deceive the poor little fishes, and spears them with the ox's horn with which his spear is shod, throwing them gasping on to the land as he catches them one by one – even so did Scylla land these panting creatures on her rock and munch them up at the mouth of her den, while they screamed and stretched out their hands to me in their mortal agony. This was the most sickening sight that I saw throughout all my voyages.

When we had passed the Wandering rocks, with Scylla and terrible Charybdis, we reached the noble island of the sun-god, where were the goodly cattle and sheep belonging to the sun Hyperion. While still at sea in my ship I could bear the cattle lowing as they came home to the yards, and the sheep bleating. Then I remembered what the blind Theban prophet Teiresias had told me, and how carefully Aeaean Circe had warned me to shun the island of the blessed sun-god. So being much troubled I said to the men, 'My men, I know you are hard pressed, but listen while I tell you the prophecy that Teiresias made me, and how carefully Aeaean Circe warned me to shun the island of the blessed sun-god, for it was here, she said, that our worst danger would lie. Head the ship, therefore, away from the island.'

The men were in despair at this, and Eurylochus at once gave me an insolent answer. 'Ulysses,' said he, 'you are cruel; you are very strong yourself and never get worn out; you seem to be made of iron, and now, though your men are exhausted with toil and want of sleep, you will not let them land and cook themselves a good supper upon this island, but bid them put out to sea and go faring fruitlessly on through the watches of the flying night. It is by night that the winds blow hardest and do so much damage; how can we escape should one of those sudden squalls spring up from South West or West, which so often wreck a vessel when our lords the gods are unpropitious? Now, therefore, let us obey the behests of night and prepare our supper here hard by the ship; to-morrow morning we will go on board again and put out to sea.'

Thus spoke Eurylochus, and the men approved his words. I saw that heaven meant us a mischief and said, 'You force me to yield, for you are many against one, but at any rate each one of you must take his solemn oath that if he meet with a herd of cattle or a large flock of sheep, he will not be so mad as to kill a single head of either, but will be satisfied with the food that Circe has given us.'

They all swore as I bade them, and when they had completed their oath we made the ship fast in a harbour that was near a stream of fresh water, and the men went ashore and cooked their suppers. As soon as they had had enough to eat and drink, they began talking about their poor comrades whom Scylla had snatched up and eaten; this set them weeping and they went on crying till they fell off into a sound sleep.

In the third watch of the night when the stars had shifted their places, Jove raised a great gale of wind that flew a hurricane so that land and sea were covered with thick clouds, and night sprang forth out of the heavens. When the child of morning, rosy-fingered Dawn, appeared, we brought the ship to land and drew her into a cave wherein the sea-nymphs hold their courts and dances, and I called the men together in council.

'My friends,' said I, 'we have meat and drink in the ship, let us mind, therefore, and not touch the cattle, or we shall suffer for it; for these cattle and sheep belong to the mighty sun, who sees and gives ear to everything.' And again they promised that they would obey.

'For a whole month the wind blew steadily from the South, and there was no other wind, but only South and East. As long as corn and wine held out the men did not touch the cattle when they were hungry; when, however, they had eaten all there was in the ship, they were forced to go further afield, with hook and line, catching birds, and taking whatever they could lay their hands on; for they were starving. One day, therefore, I went up inland that I might pray heaven to show me some means of getting away. When I had gone far enough to be clear of all my men, and had found a place that was well sheltered from the wind, I washed my hands and prayed to all the gods in Olympus till by and by they sent me off into a sweet sleep.

Meanwhile Eurylochus had been giving evil counsel to the men, 'Listen to me,' said he, 'my poor comrades. All deaths are bad enough but there is none so bad as famine. Why should not we drive in the best of these cows and offer them in sacrifice to the immortal gods? If we ever get back to Ithaca, we can build a fine temple to the sun-god and enrich it with every kind of ornament; if, however, he is determined to sink our ship out of revenge for these horned cattle, and the other gods are of the same mind, I for one would rather drink salt water once for all and have done with it, than be starved to death by inches in such a desert island as this is.'

Thus spoke Eurylochus, and the men approved his words. Now the cattle, so fair and goodly, were feeding not far from the ship; the men, therefore, drove in the best of them, and they all stood round them saying their prayers, and using young oak-shoots instead of barley-meal, for there was no barley left. When they had done praying they killed the cows and dressed their carcasses; they cut out the thigh bones, wrapped them round in two layers of fat, and set some pieces of raw meat on top of them. They had no wine with which to make drink-offerings over the sacrifice while it was cooking, so they kept pouring on a little water from time to time while the inward meats were being grilled; then, when the thigh bones were burned and they had tasted the inward meats, they cut the rest up small and put the pieces upon the spits.

By this time my deep sleep had left me, and I turned back to the ship and to the sea shore. As I drew near I began to smell hot roast meat, so I groaned out a prayer to the immortal gods. 'Father Jove,' I exclaimed, 'and all you other gods who live in everlasting bliss, you have done me a cruel mischief by the sleep into which you have sent me; see what fine work these men of mine have been making in my absence.'

Meanwhile Lampetie went straight off to the sun and told him we had been killing his cows, whereon he flew into a great rage, and said to the immortals, 'Father Jove, and all you other gods who live in everlasting bliss, I must have vengeance on the crew of Ulysses' ship: they have had the insolence to kill my cows, which were the one thing I loved to look upon, whether I was going up heaven or down again. If they do not square accounts with me about my cows, I will go down to Hades and shine there among the dead.'

'Sun,' said Jove, 'go on shining upon us gods and upon mankind over the fruitful earth. I will shiver their ship into little pieces with a bolt of white lightning as soon as they get out to sea.'

I was told all this by Calypso, who said she had heard it from the mouth of Mercury.

As soon as I got down to my ship and to the sea shore I rebuked each one of the men separately, but we could see no way out of it, for the cows were dead already. And indeed the gods began at once to show signs and wonders among us, for the hides of the cattle crawled about, and the joints upon the spits began to low like cows, and the meat, whether cooked or raw, kept on making a noise just as cows do.

For six days my men kept driving in the best cows and feasting upon them, but when Jove the son of Saturn had added a seventh day, the fury of the gale abated; we therefore went on board, raised our masts, spread sail, and put out to sea. As soon as we were well away from the island, and could see nothing but sky and sea, the son of Saturn raised a black cloud over our ship, and the sea grew dark beneath it. We did not get on much further, for in another moment we were caught by a terrific squall from the West that snapped the forestays of the mast so that it fell aft, while all the ship's gear tumbled about at the bottom of the vessel. The mast fell upon the head of the helmsman in the ship's stern, so that the bones of his head were crushed to pieces, and he fell overboard as though he were diving, with no more life left in him.

Then Jove let fly with his thunderbolts, and the ship went round and round, and was filled with fire and brimstone as the lightning struck it. The men all fell into the sea; they were carried about in the water round the ship, looking like so many sea-gulls, but the god presently deprived them of all chance of getting home again.

I stuck to the ship till the sea knocked her sides from her keel (which drifted about by itself) and struck the mast out of her in the direction of the keel; but there was a backstay of stout ox-thong still hanging about it, and with this I lashed the mast and keel together, and getting astride of them was carried wherever the winds chose to take me.

The gale from the West had now spent its force, and the wind got into the South again, which frightened me lest I should be taken back to the terrible whirlpool of Charybdis. This indeed was what actually happened, for I was borne along by the waves all night, and by sunrise had reached the rock of Scylla, and the whirlpool. She was then sucking down the salt sea water, but I was carried aloft toward the fig tree, which I caught hold of and clung on to like a bat. I could not plant my feet anywhere so as to stand securely, for the roots were a long way off and the boughs that overshadowed the whole pool were too high, too vast, and too far apart for me to reach them; so I hung patiently on, waiting till the pool should discharge my mast and raft again – and a very long while it seemed. A jury-man is not more glad to get home to supper, after having been long detained in court by troublesome cases, than I was to see my raft beginning to work its way out of the whirlpool again. At last I let go with my hands and feet, and fell heavily into the sea, hard by my raft on to which I then got, and began to row with my hands. As for Scylla, the father of gods and men would not let her get further sight of me – otherwise I should have certainly been lost.

Hence I was carried along for nine days till on the tenth night the gods stranded me on the Ogygian island, where dwells the great and powerful goddess Calypso. She took me in and was kind to me, but I need say no more about this, for I told you and your noble wife all about it yesterday, and I hate saying the same thing over and over again.

MERMAIDS & MERMEN

They had beautiful voices, far finer than any human being's
— Hans Christian Andersen

from
THE MERMAN AND THE FIGURE-HEAD

CLARA F GUERNSEY

The figure-head of the Sea-nymph was carried through the streets in the midst of an admiring throng and fixed securely in its place on the beautiful new brig. A few days more, and the ship was launched and slid swiftly and safely into the sea. That night it was bright moonlight. Silver-gilt ripples were rising and falling along the coast and all over the bay. Now and then a fish would jump, scattering a shower of shining drops. Everything was very still around the Sea-nymph. She lay quite by herself at some distance from any other craft. There was no one on board but an old watchman, who was fast asleep. If he had been awake, he would have seen a long, bright ripple on the water coming nearer as some sea creature cut its way swiftly toward the new craft. It was our merman, who found himself drawn toward the land by a longing curiosity too strong for him to resist.

'It is all so quiet and still,' he thought. 'There can be no possible danger, and I do so want to see what sort of houses these human creatures live in. There's a new ship. I'm a great mind to go and look at it. What is that standing there on the end of it?'

The merman swam on slowly, debating whether he should really go and look. Something seemed at once to warn him away and to call him forward. He could not tell what was the matter with him. Once he turned to swim away. Then he made up his mind once for all, and dashed straight on toward the ship. He said over to himself a charm his grandfather had taught him: 'Aski, kataski, lix tetrax, damnamenous,' words of power once written on the fish-bodied statue of the great goddess of Ephesus; but, dear me! it did him no good at all. All the while he was coming the wooden nymph stood up in her place, holding out her silver vase in both hands and looking over the sea with her painted eyes.

'What a lovely creature!' thought the merman. 'She is looking at me; she holds her vase toward me.'

She was doing no such thing, of course – the wooden image – but he thought she was. He did not know that she would have looked just the same way if he had been an old porpoise instead of a young merman. He swam closer and closer. The moon shone on the painted face. The ship moved gently on the water. The merman thought the lady had inclined her head. In one moment he fell desperately, helplessly, in love with the oaken nymph. It certainly must have been the doing of the old Witch of the Sea. Some influence of the kind must have been at work, or else a merman who had been to college would surely have had more sense than to become enamored of an oak block. But whether it was the witch's work, or whether it was the drop of human blood in his veins, or whether it was fate, that is just what he did – he fell in love with a wooden image. He forgot his home, his old grandfather, his sisters, his best friend, who loved him like a brother and who had saved his life in the war. As for the mermaid who had given him the ring, he never gave her a thought. He didn't care for anything in the world but that painted image smiling up there and holding its vase. He saw nothing but that, and, in fact, he didn't see that either, for he saw it as if it were alive.

'Oh I wish I knew her name or what she is!' said the merman to himself. 'She can't be human. She is too beautiful.' He swam round and round and read the words 'The Sea-nymph' painted under the figure. He gave a jump almost out of the water. 'It is a nymph,' he said – 'one of the Nereides or Oceanides. I thought they had left this world long ago. What can she be doing on that ship?'

He gazed at the wooden creature with all his heart in his eyes. He wished he were human that he might at least be a little like this lovely shape. He hated his own form. Was it likely the divine nymph would ever deign to notice a creature with a fish's tail? Finally he ventured to speak.

'Fairest nymph,' he said.

He got no answer, but as the shadow of a cloud flitted across her face, and then the moon shone on her, he thought the nymph smiled. If there had been any possible way, he would certainly have climbed up to her, though he knew he could not live five minutes out of the water. He did not think anything about that, the poor silly merman. He was so infatuated that he would have been glad to die beside her. He stayed there the whole night talking to the wooden sea-nymph, and when the image moved with the rise and fall of the water he thought she inclined her head toward him. He said the most extravagant things to her; he told her all he had ever thought or felt, things he had never spoken to his best friend who loved him dearly; he poured out all his heart into the deaf ears of the wooden nymph. The image kept looking out over the water with its painted eyes, and the merman thought, 'Now at last I have found some one who can understand me.'

It was growing to gray dawn when a huge sea gull came sweeping over the water, and poised and hovered over the merman's head.

'Hallo!' said the sea-gull to the merman, 'what are you up to, young man?'

The merman was disgusted and made no answer.

'You'd better clear out of this,' said the gull. 'If they catch you, they'll make a show of you and wheel you round the streets in a tub of water for sixpence a sight.'

'Be so good as to reserve your anxiety for your own affairs,' said the merman, haughtily. He had always been sweet-tempered, but now he felt as if he must have a quarrel with some one. He had a general impression that every living creature was his rival and enemy. He didn't just know what he wanted, but he was determined to have it.

'Highty tighty!' said the sea-gull. 'Don't put yourself out. What have we here? A pretty wooden image, upon my word!' and the gull perched on the sea-nymph's head and scratched his ear with one claw. The merman went almost wild at the sight.

'You profane wretch!' he shouted; 'how dare you? Oh, good heavens, that I should see her so insulted and not be able to help her. Oh, why can't I fly?'

'Cause you hain't got no wings,' said the vulgar bird, flapping his own wide white pinions. 'Why shouldn't I perch here as well as on any other post? It's none of your funeral.'

'Post!' said the merman, in a fury.

'Yes, post! Why? You don't mean to say you think this thing's alive?'

'Alive! She is a goddess, a nymph, an angel!'

'Well, you are a muff,' said the gull, with immense contempt. 'If I ever! Look here! if you don't want a harpoon in you, you had better quit.'

'I'll wring your neck,' said the merman, in a rage.

'Skee-ee-eek!' screamed the gull. 'Will you have it now or wait till you get it? Take your own way, if you only know what it is;' and the gull lifted his wings and swept off over the water, laughing frantically. The wooden lady kept looking over the sea.

'What noble composure! what breeding!' thought the

merman. 'She scorns to notice a creature like that. How much more noble and womanly is this modest reserve and silence than the chatter and laughing of our mermaids!'

It grew lighter and lighter; sounds of life were heard from the shore; a boat put out on the bay; presently the workmen began to come on board the brig.

'Any of those human beings can speak to her,' thought the merman. He was frantically jealous of an old ship carpenter with a wooden leg.

One of the workmen caught a glimpse of him. 'Ho!' said he, 'there's an odd fish! Who's got a harpoon?'

The merman had just sense enough left to see that if he was harpooned in the morning he couldn't court the goddess at night. He dived and swam away, for mermen, although they are warm-blooded animals, are not obliged to come up to the top of the water to breathe.

He hid all day long under the timbers of an old wharf, and when it was still at night he came out again and swam toward The Sea-nymph. Some one had covered up the figure with an old sheet to keep the dust off. The merman thought she had put on a veil.

'What charming modesty!' he said. 'She don't wish to be seen by these human beings, or perhaps I offended her by my staring.'

He called her every lovely name he could invent or think of. He got no answer, of course, but that was her feminine reserve, the merman thought.

'Speech is silvern, silence is golden,' he said. So it went on all the time the new brig was being fitted up. The merman lived a wretched life. Two or three times he was seen and chased by the fishermen. A talk went about of the odd creature that haunted the water near the new ship. Some one was always on the lookout for him, and once he was nearly caught. They kept watch for him at night. It was only now and then that he could worship his wooden love for an hour.

All the time the old sheet was over her head, but the merman only loved her the better. He hid under the old wharf by day, for though he knew how to make himself invisible to mermen, the charm hadn't the slightest effect where Yankees were concerned. He lived on whatever he could catch, but he had very little appetite. The shallow harbor water did not agree with his constitution. He grew thin and hollow-eyed, a mere ghost of a merman, but he was constant to his wooden image.

Meantime, the ship was finished and the cargo was stowed away. One day, glancing out from his place, he saw that the nymph was unveiled and was standing in her old fashion, lovely as ever. She was looking straight at him, the merman thought. 'She is anxious about my safety,' he said, with delight, for he did not know that the image just looked toward the old wharf because it happened to be in the way.

'Dearest,' he said, 'I would follow you over the whole ocean for such a look as that!'

That night there were so many men on board the brig that the merman did not dare go near her. The next morning the ship spread her sails and went out of the harbor with a fair wind, bound for Lisbon and the Mediterranean. That same evening there was a great gathering at Colonel Shuttleworth's. Master Torrey was married to Anna Jane.

The merman followed the ship at a long distance. He dared not go too near in the daytime for fear of the harpoon that had been thrown at him once or twice. Then it came into his head that the lovely nymph was in some mysterious way held captive by these human creatures. He swore to deliver her if it cost him his life, for which he cared only as it could serve his goddess, for that she was a goddess he fully believed.

He swam in the wake of the ship, and it was very seldom that he could come up and look his idol in the face. The sailors kept a sharp lookout for him. They thought he was some sort of monster, the poor innocent merman, and had harpoons ready to throw at him whenever he showed himself. But for all this he followed The Sea-nymph across the Atlantic. He knew he was not likely to meet any of his own people, for the merfolk avoid ships whenever they can, and do not frequent the highway between the two continents.

One day, however, he was so possessed with a desire for the sight of his love that, utterly reckless, he swam directly before the ship and stretched out his arms to the wooden image. 'I am here! I will die for you!' he cried, for he thought she was suffering in her captivity and wanted comfort. There was a shout from the sailors; one flung a fish spear, another fired a gun. The captain ordered out the whale-boat, and they gave chase to the merman, for such they now saw it was. It was all that he could do to get away. He was a very fast swimmer, however, and as he was not obliged to come up to breathe, they soon lost sight of him. He distanced the boat, but he found when he stopped that the bullet from the gun had grazed his shoulder, and that he had lost blood and was suffering pain. 'It is for her,' thought the merman as he tried to stanch the blood with his pocket handkerchief.

Just then a huge sperm whale came dashing up.

'Why, what in the world are you doing here?' said the whale, surprised. 'Have those wretches of men been chasing you?'

'Yes,' said the merman, his eyes flashing; 'you may well call them wretches. Do you know who it is they hold prisoner in their hateful ship? The loveliest sea-nymph in the world.'

'How do you know?' said the whale.

'I have seen her. I have followed her all the way from home. She stands holding out a silver vase. Every creature in the sea ought to fly to deliver her. If I was only as big and strong as you! These men are your enemies as well as mine and hers. I know how they kill you whales whenever they can. You can sink that ship if you like and deliver the goddess.'

The whale was so astonished that he had to go to the top of the water and blow. 'My dear sir,' said he, diving down again, 'you are under some strange mistake. That is nothing but wood, that figure on the ship, as sure as my name is Moby Dick.'

'You great stupid creature, where are your eyes?' said the merman in a passion, and yet he was rather struck by the whale's remarks too.

'In my head,' said Moby Dick, 'and I shouldn't think yours were. Why they put some such thing on all the ships – women, dolphins, what not. I've seen dozens of 'em. I know about nymphs. I used to read about 'em in the old classical dictionary in our school. Every school of whales of any pretension has one. If she was a sea goddess, do you suppose she'd stand there in all weathers? Besides, there are no nymphs.'

'Then you won't sink the ship?' said the merman.

'Certainly not; she's only a merchant ship. If she was a whaler, I would with pleasure. I've done it before now, but that was in self-defence. I'm not going to drown a lot of folks because you have lost your wits. Come, come, my young friend, go home to your family. I dare say your mother don't know you're out. You are too tired to swim after that ship, and you are hurt besides. Let me take you home on my back; I'd just as soon swim your way as any other.'

The merman was a little affected by the whale's tone of kindness, but he was too much possessed with his wooden love to accept the offer.

'No! no!' he cried, 'I must follow her to the ends of the earth. Something tells me she will yet be mine.'

'And suppose she should be?' said Moby Dick. 'Why, she's only a stick cut and painted. What would the ladies of your family think if you brought home a wooden wife?'

'You are blind,' said the merman, swimming away.

'You are cracked!' the whale shouted after him, but the merman was already out of hearing.

'Dear! dear!' said Moby Dick. 'What a pity! If I can find any of the mermen, I'll tell them about him. He ought not to be left to himself;' and he shook his huge head solemnly and swam away in an opposite direction.

O SWIFTLY GLIDES THE BONNY BOAT

JOHANNA BAILEY

O swiftly glides the bonny boat
Just parted from the shore:
And to the fisher's chorus note,
Soft moves the dipping oar.
These toils are borne with happy cheer,
And ever may they speed,
That feeble age and helpmates dear,
And tender bairnies feed.

We cast our lines in Largo Bay,
Our nets are floating wide;
Our bonny boat with yielding sway,
Rocks lightly on the tide;
And happy prove our daily lot,
Upon the summer sea!
And blest on land our kindly cot,
Where all our treasures be!

The mermaid on her rock may sing,
The witch may weave her charm;
Nor water-sprite, nor eldrich thing,
The bonny boat can harm:
It safely bears its scaly store,
Through many a stormy gale;
While joyful shouts rise from the shore,
Its homeward prow to hail.

THE MERMAN

ALFRED, LORD TENNYSON

Who would be
A merman bold,
Sitting alone,
Singing alone
Under the sea,
With a crown of gold,
On a throne?

I would be a merman bold;
I would sit and sing the whole of the day;
I would fill the sea-halls with a voice of power;
But at night I would roam abroad and play
With the mermaids in and out of the rocks,
Dressing their hair with the white sea-flower;
And holding them back by their flowing locks
I would kiss them often under the sea,
And kiss them again till they kiss'd me
Laughingly, laughingly;
And then we would wander away, away
To the pale-green sea-groves straight and high,
Chasing each other merrily.

There would be neither moon nor star;
But the wave would make music above us afar–
Low thunder and light in the magic night–
Neither moon nor star.
We would call aloud in the dreamy dells,
Call to each other and whoop and cry
All night, merrily, merrily;
They would pelt me with starry spangles and shells,
Laughing and clapping their hands between,
All night, merrily, merrily:
But I would throw to them back in mine
Turkis and agate and almondine:

Then leaping out upon them unseen
I would kiss them often under the sea,
And kiss them again till they kiss'd me
Laughingly, laughingly.
Oh! what a happy life were mine
Under the hollow-hung ocean green!
Soft are the moss-beds under the sea;
We would live merrily, merrily.

from
A VISION OF MERMAIDS

GERARD MANLEY HOPKINS

So those Mermaidens crowded to my rock,
And thicken'd, like that drifted bloom, the flock
Sun-flush'd, until it seem'd their father Sea
Had gotten him a wreath of sweet Spring-broidery.
Careless of me they sported: some would plash
The languent smooth with dimpling drops, and flash
Their filmy tails adown whose length there show'd
An azure ridge; or clouds of violet glow'd
On pranked scale; or threads of carmine, shot
Thro' silver, gloom'd to a blood-vivid clot.
Some, diving merrily, downward drove, and gleam'd
With arm and fin; the argent bubbles stream'd
Airwards, disturb'd; and the scarce troubled sea
Gurgled, where they had sunk, melodiously.
Others with fingers white would comb among
The drenched hair of slabby weeds that swung
Swimming, and languish'd green upon the deep
Down that dank rock o'er which their lush long tresses weep.

But most in a half-circle watch'd the sun;
And a sweet sadness dwelt on everyone;
I knew not why, – but know that sadness dwells
On Mermaids – whether that they ring the knells
Of seamen whelm'd in chasms of the mid-main,
As poets sing; or that it is a pain
To know the dusk depths of the ponderous sea,
The miles profound of solid green, and be
With loath'd cold fishes, far from man – or what; –
I know the sadness but the cause know not.
Then they, thus ranged, 'gan make full plaintively
A piteous Siren sweetness on the sea,
Withouten instrument, or conch, or bell,
Or stretch'd chords tuneable on turtle's shell;
Only with utterance of sweet breath they sung
An antique chaunt and in an unknown tongue.

THE MERMAID

ALFRED, LORD TENNYSON

Who would be
A mermaid fair,
Singing alone,
Combing her hair
Under the sea,
In a golden curl
With a comb of pearl,
On a throne?

I would be a mermaid fair;
I would sing to myself the whole of the day;
With a comb of pearl I would comb my hair;
And still as I comb'd I would sing and say,
'Who is it loves me? who loves not me?'
I would comb my hair till my ringlets would fall,
Low adown, low adown,
From under my starry sea-bud crown
Low adown and around,
And I should look like a fountain of gold
Springing alone
With a shrill inner sound,
Over the throne
In the midst of the hall;
Till that great sea-snake under the sea
From his coiled sleeps in the central deeps
Would slowly trail himself sevenfold
Round the hall where I sate, and look in at the gate
With his large calm eyes for the love of me.
And all the mermen under the sea
Would feel their immortality
Die in their hearts for the love of me.

But at night I would wander away, away,
I would fling on each side my low-flowing locks,
And lightly vault from the throne and play
With the mermen in and out of the rocks;
We would run to and fro, and hide and seek,
On the broad sea-wolds in the crimson shells,
Whose silvery spikes are nighest the sea.
But if any came near I would call, and shriek,
And adown the steep like a wave I would leap
From the diamond-ledges that jut from the dells;
For I would not be kiss'd by all who would list,
Of the bold merry mermen under the sea;
They would sue me, and woo me, and flatter me,
In the purple twilights under the sea;
But the king of them all would carry me,
Woo me, and win me, and marry me,
In the branching jaspers under the sea;
Then all the dry pied things that be
In the hueless mosses under the sea
Would curl round my silver feet silently,
All looking up for the love of me.
And if I should carol aloud, from aloft
All things that are forked, and horned, and soft
Would lean out from the hollow sphere of the sea,
All looking down for the love of me.

CAPE HORN GOSPEL

JOHN MASEFIELD

'I was in a hooker once,' said Karlssen,
'And Bill, as was a seaman, died,
So we lashed him in an old tarpaulin
And tumbled him across the side;
And the fun of it was that all his gear was
Divided up among the crew
Before that blushing human error,
Our crawling little captain, knew.

'On the passage home one morning
(As certain as I prays for grace)
There was old Bill's shadder a-hauling
At the weather mizzen-topsail brace.
He was all grown green with sea-weed,
He was all lashed up and shored;
So I says to him, I says, "Why, Billy!
What's a-bringin' of you back aboard?"

'"I'm a-weary of them there mermaids,"
Says old Bill's ghost to me;
"It ain't no place for a Christian
Below there – under sea.
For it's all blown sand and shipwrecks,
And old bones eaten bare,
And them cold fishy females
With long green weeds for hair.

‘And there ain’t no dances shuffled,
And no old yarns is spun,
And there ain’t no stars but starfish,
And never any moon or sun.
I heard your keel a-passing
And the running rattle of the brace,”
And he says, “Stand by,” says William,
“For a shift towards a better place.”

‘Well, he sogered about decks till sunrise,
When a rooster in the hen-coop crowed,
And as so much smoke he faded
And as so much smoke he goed;
And I’ve often wondered since, Jan,
How his old ghost stands to fare
Long o’ them cold fishy females
With long green weeds for hair.’

THE MERMAID

W B YEATS

A mermaid found a swimming lad,
Picked him for her own,
Pressed her body to his body,
Laughed; and plunging down
Forgot in cruel happiness
That even lovers drown.

THE SEA SPIRIT

LUCY MAUD MONTGOMERY

I smile o'er the wrinkled blue–
Lo! the sea is fair,
Smooth as the flow of a maiden's hair;
And the welkin's light shines through
Into mid-sea caverns of beryl hue,
And the little waves laugh and the mermaids sing,
And the sea is a beautiful, sinuous thing!

I scowl in sullen guise–
The sea grows dark and dun,
The swift clouds hide the sun
But not the bale-light in my eyes,
And the frightened wind as it flies
Ruffles the billows with stormy wing,
And the sea is a terrible, treacherous thing!

When moonlight glimmers dim
I pass in the path of the mist,
Like a pale spirit by spirits kissed.
At dawn I chant my own weird hymn,
And I dabble my hair in the sunset's rim,
And I call to the dwellers along the shore
With a voice of gramarye evermore.

And if one for love of me
Gives to my call an ear,
I will woo him and hold him dear,
And teach him the way of the sea,
And my glamor shall ever over him be;
Though he wander afar in the cities of men
He will come at last to my arms again.

from A MIDSUMMER NIGHT'S DREAM

WILLIAM SHAKESPEARE

Oberon: My gentle Puck, come hither. Thou rememb'rest
Since once I sat upon a promontory
And heard a mermaid on a dolphin's back
Uttering such dulcet and harmonious breath
That the rude sea grew civil at her song
And certain stars shot madly from their spheres
To hear the sea-maid's music.

Robin: I remember.

MERMAID

FRANCIS JAMES CHILD

As we lay musing in our beds,
So well and so warm at ease,
I thought upon those lodging-beds
Poor seamen have at seas.

Last Easter day, in the morning fair,
We was not far from land,
Where we spied a mermaid on the rock,
With comb and glass in hand.

The first came up the mate of our ship,
With lead and line in hand,
To sound and see how deep we was
From any rock or sand.

The next came up the boatswain of our ship,
With courage stout and bold:
'Stand fast, stand fast, my brave lively lads,
Stand fast, my brave hearts of gold!'

Our gallant ship is gone to wreck,
Which was so lately trimmd;
The raging seas has sprung a leak,
And the salt water does run in.

Our gold and silver, and all our cloths,
And all that ever we had,
We forced was to heave them overboard,
Thinking our lives to save.

In all, the number that was on board
Was five hundred and sixty-four,
And all that ever came alive on shore
There was but poor ninety-five.

The first bespoke the captain of our ship,
And a well-spoke man was he;
'I have a wife in fair Plymouth town,
And a widow I fear she must be.'

The next bespoke the mate of our ship,
And a well-bespoke man was he;
'I have a wife in fair Portsmouth,
And a widow I fear she must be.'

The next bespoke the boatswain of our ship,
And a well-bespoke man was he;
'I have a wife in fair Exeter,
And a widow I fear she must be.'

The next bespoke the little cabbin-boy,
And a well-bespoke boy was he;
'I am as sorry for my mother dear
As you are for your wives all three.

'Last night, when the moon shin'd bright,
My mother had sons five,
But now she may look in the salt seas
And find but one alive.'

'Call a boat, call a boat, you little Plymouth boys,
Don't you hear how the trumpets sound?
For the want of our boat our gallant ship is lost,
And the most of our merry men is drownd.'

Whilst the raging seas do roar,
And the lofty winds do blow,
And we poor seamen do lie on the top,
Whilst the landmen lies below.

A MERMAID'S SONG

ANNE HUNTER

Now the dancing sunbeams play
On the green and glassy sea,
Come, and I will lead the way
Where the pearly treasures be.
Come with me, and we will go
Where the rocks of coral grow.
Follow, follow, follow me.

Come, behold what treasures lie
Far below the rolling waves,
Riches, hid from human eye,
Dimly shine in ocean's caves.
Ebbing tides bear no delay,
Stormy winds are far away.

MOTHER CAREY
(AS TOLD ME BY THE BO'SUN)

JOHN MASEFIELD

Mother Carey? She's the mother o' the witches
'N' all them sort o' rips;
She's a fine gell to look at, but the hitch is,
She's a sight too fond of ships.
She lives upon a iceberg to the norred,
'N' her man he's Davy Jones,
'N' she combs the weeds upon her forred
With pore drowned sailors' bones.

She's the mother o' the wrecks, 'n' the mother
Of all big winds as blows;
She's up to some deviltry or other
When it storms, or sleets, or snows.
The noise of the wind's her screamin',
'I'm arter a plump, young, fine,
Brass-buttoned, beefy-ribbed young seam'n
So as me 'n' my mate kin dine.'

She's a hungry old rip 'n' a cruel
For sailor-men like we,
She's give a many mariners the gruel
'N' a long sleep under sea.
She's the blood o' many a crew upon her
'N' the bones of many a wreck,
'N' she's barnacles a-growin' on her
'N' shark's teeth round her neck.

I ain't never had no schoolin'
Nor read no books like you,
But I knows 't ain't healthy to be foolin'
With that there gristly two.
You're young, you thinks, 'n' you're lairy,
But if you're to make old bones,
Steer clear, I says, o' Mother Carey,
'N' that there Davy Jones.

from THE MERMAID

JOHN LEYDEN

The moonbeams crisp the curling surge,
That streaks with foam the ocean green;
While forward still the rowers urge
Their course, a female form was seen.

That sea-maid's form, of pearly light,
Was whiter than the downy spray,
And round her bosom, heaving bright,
Her glossy, yellow ringlets play.

Borne on a foamy-crested wave,
She reached amain the bounding prow,
Then, clasping fast the chieftain brave,
She, plunging, sought the deep below,

Ah! long beside thy feigned bier,
The monks the prayers of death shall say,
And long for thee, the fruitless tear
Shall weep the maid of Colonsay!

But downwards, like a powerless corse,
The eddying waves the chieftain bear;
He only heard the moaning hoarse
Of waters, murmuring in his ear.

The murmurs sink, by slow degrees;
No more the surges round him rave;
Lulled by the music of the seas,
He lies within a coral cave.

THE MERMAID

JAMES GATES PERCIVAL

The waning moon looked cold and pale,
Just rising o'er the eastern wave,
And faintly moaned the evening gale,
That swept along the gloomy cave:
The waves that wildly rose and fell,
On all the rocks the white foam flung,
And like the distant funeral knell,
Within her grot the Mermaid sung.

It was a strain of witchery
So sweet, yet mournful to my ear,
It lit the smile, it waked the sigh,
Then started pity's pearly tear;
There was a ruffle in my breast,
It was not joy, it was not pain,
'T was wild as yonder billow's crest,
That tosses o'er the heaving main.

Along the wave the moon's cold light
With trembling radiance feebly shone;
A lustre neither faint nor bright
Sparkled on yonder watery stone:
There, seated on her sea-beat throne,
The Mermaid eyed the dashing wave,
Then waked her wild harp's melting tone,
And breathed the music of the grave.

Her silken tresses, all unbound,
Played loosely on the evening gale;
She cast a mournful look around,
Then sweetly woke her wild harp's wail;
And, as her marble fingers flew
Along the chords, such music flowed,
Her cheek assumed a varied hue,
Where grief grew pale, where pleasure glowed.

The sound rose sweetly on the wind,
It was a strain of melancholy,–
It soothed each tumult of the mind,
And hushed the wildest laugh of folly.
It flowed so softly o'er the main,
And spread so calmly, widely 'round;
The air seemed living with the strain,
And every zephyr breathed the sound.

The seal, that sported on the shore,
His gambols ceased, and pricked his ear;
He heeded not the billow's roar,–
That strain was all he seemed to hear.
As through the surf the dolphins flew,
They stopped and played around her throne;
It seemed, Arion woke anew
His harp to some celestial tone.

With what a thrilling ecstasy
I heard the music of her lyre;
The very soul of melody
Seemed warbling on the trembling wire:
O, never o'er her infant dear
The mother half so fondly hung,
As when I bent my soul to hear
Those heavenly strains the Mermaid sung.

from
THE LITTLE MERMAID

HANS CHRISTIAN ANDERSEN

Far out in the sea the water is as blue as the petals of the loveliest of cornflowers, and as clear as the clearest glass; but it is very deep, deeper than any anchor-cable can reach, and many church towers would have to be put one on the top of another to reach from the bottom out of the water. Down there live the sea people.

Now you must not think for a moment that there is only a bare white sandy bottom there; no, no: there the most extraordinary trees and plants grow, which have stems and leaves so supple that they stir at the slightest movement of the water, as if they were alive. All the fish, big and little, flit among the branches, like the birds in the air up here. In the deepest place of all lies the sea king's palace. The walls are of coral, and the tall pointed windows of the clearest possible amber, but the roof is of mussel-shells that open and shut themselves as the water moves. It all looks beautiful, for in every one of them lie shining pearls, a single one of which would be the principal ornament in a Queen's crown.

The sea King down there had been a widower for many years, but his old mother kept house for him. She was a clever woman, but proud of her rank, for which reason she went about with twelve oysters on her tail, while the rest of the nobility might only carry six. For the rest she deserved high praise, especially because she was so fond of the little sea Princesses, her grandchildren.

There were six of them, beautiful children, but the youngest was the prettiest of them all. Her skin was as bright and pure as a rose-leaf, her eyes were as blue as the deepest lake; but like all the rest, she had no feet – her body ended in a fish's tail. All the love-long day they might play down in the palace in the great halls where live flowers grew out of the walls. The big windows of amber stood open, and the fishes swam in through them, just as with us swallows fly in when we open the windows; but the fishes used to swim right up to the little Princesses and feed out of their hands and allow themselves to be stroked.

Outside the palace there was a large garden with fiery red and dark blue trees, whose fruit shone like gold, and their flowers were like a flaming fire, because they were always moving their stems and leaves. The ground was of the finest sand, but blue like the flame of sulphur. Over the whole expanse down there lay a wonderful blue sheen. You could more easily imagine that you were far up in the air and could see the sky above you and below you, than that you were at the bottom of the sea. In a dead calm you could see the sun: it looked like a purple flower out of whose cup all the light was streaming.

Each of the young Princesses had her little plot in the garden, where she could dig and plant as she liked. One would make her flower-bed in the shape of a whale, another preferred to have hers like a little mermaid, but the youngest made hers quite round, like the sun, and would only have flowers that shone red like it. She was an odd child, quiet and thoughtful, and whereas the other sisters would deck out their gardens with the quaintest things, that they had got from sunken ships, she would only have – besides the rose-red flowers that were like the sun far up in the sky – a pretty statue of marble. It was of a handsome boy, carved out of bright white stone, which had come down to the sea bottom from a wreck. Beside the statue she planted a rose-red weeping willow, which grew splendidly and hung its fresh branches over it, right down to the blue sand bottom, on which the shadows showed violet, and moved with the branches; it looked as if the top and the roots of the tree were playing at kissing each other.

She had no greater delight than in dreaming about the world of men up above. The old grandmother had to tell her all she knew about ships and horses and men and animals. It seemed to her particularly delightful that up there on earth the flowers smelt sweet (which they did not at the sea bottom), and that the woods were green and the fish which one saw among the branches could sing so loud and prettily that it was a joy to hear them. It was the little birds that the grandmother called fish, otherwise they could not have understood, for they had never seen a bird.

'When you're full fifteen years old,' said the grandmother, 'you shall have leave to come up out of the sea and sit on the rocks in the moonlight, and see the big ships that come sailing by; and forests and houses you shall see.'

During the year that was passing one of the sisters was fifteen years old; but the rest – why, each was a year younger than the next, and so the youngest had a clear five years to wait before she could come up from the sea bottom and see how things go with us. But the first promised the next one to tell her what she had seen and had thought beautiful on the first day, for their grandmother didn't tell them enough: there were very many things they wanted to know about.

None of them was so full of longing as the youngest, the very one who had the longest time to wait, and was so quiet and thoughtful. Many a night she stood at the open window and gazed up through the dark blue waters where the fish went waving their fins and tails. She could see the moon and the stars; of course they were very pale, but, seen through the water, they looked much larger than they do to our eyes. If something like a black cloud passed along beneath them, she knew that it was either a whale swimming above her, or even a ship with a number of people in it. Certainly they never thought that beneath them there was a lovely little mermaid stretching her hands up towards the keel.

And now the eldest Princess was fifteen years old and could rise up above the surface of the sea.

When she came back she had a hundred things to tell; but the most beautiful thing, she said, was to lie on a sandbank in the moonlight in the calm sea, and to see close by the shore the big town where the lights twinkled like hundreds of stars, and to hear the sound of music and the noise and stir of carts and people, and see all the church towers and steeples and hear the bells ringing; and just because she couldn't go up there, she longed after all that, most of all.

Oh, how the youngest sister did listen! And when, later on in the evening, she stood at the open window and gazed up through the dark blue water, she thought about the big town and all the noise and stir, and then she fancied she could hear the church bells ringing down to her.

The year after, the second sister had leave to rise up through the water and swim where she liked; she ducked up just as the sun was going down, and the sight of that she thought the most beautiful of all. The whole heaven, she said, had looked like gold, and the clouds – oh! the beauty of them she could not describe: red and violet, they sailed past above her, but far swifter than they there flew, like a large white ribbon, a skein of wild swans away over the water, to where the sun was. She swam towards it, but it sank, and the rosy glow died from the clouds and the face of the sea.

Next year the third sister went up; she was the boldest of them all; and so she swam up a broad river that ran into the sea. Beautiful green hills she saw, with rows of vines upon them. Palaces and mansions peeped out from among stately woods. She heard all the birds singing, and the sun shone so hot that she had to dive beneath the water to cool her burning face. In a little inlet she came upon a whole crowd of young human children; they were quite naked, and ran about and splashed in the water. She wanted to play with them, but they ran away in a fright, and then came a little black creature (it was a dog, but she had never seen a dog before) and it barked at her so dreadfully that she was terrified and took refuge in the open sea; but never could she forget the splendid woods and the green hills and the pretty children who could swim in the water, though they had no fish-tails.

The fourth sister was not so daring. She stayed out in the lonely sea, and told them that that was the most beautiful of all. You could see many many miles all round, and the sky arched over you like a great bell of glass. Ships she had seen, but far away they looked like gulls. The merry dolphins had turned somersaults, and the big whales had squirted up water out of their nostrils, so that it looked like hundreds of fountains all around her.

Now came the turn of the fifth sister. Her birthday, it happened, was in winter, and so she saw what the others had not seen on their first visit. The sea was all green to look at, and round about there floated large icebergs, every one looking like a pearl, she said, and yet they were far bigger than the church towers that men built. They showed themselves in the strangest shapes and were like diamonds. She had seated herself on one of the largest, and all the ships made a wide circle in fear, away from the place where she was sitting and letting the wind set her long hair flying; but on towards evening the sky was covered with clouds, it lightened and thundered, while the black sea lifted the masses of ice high up, and made them glitter in the fierce lightning. Aboard of all the ships they took in sail, and there was anxiety and fear, but she sat calmly on her floating iceberg and watched the blue flashes strike zig-zagging into the shining sea.

The first time any of the sisters came to the top of the water, each one of them was always entranced by all the new pretty sights she saw, but now that, as grown girls, they had leave to go up whenever they liked, it became quite ordinary to them, and they longed to be at home again; and after a month had passed they said that after all it was far prettier down at the bottom, and there one was so comfortable at home.

On many an evening the five sisters would link arms together and rise in a row above the water. They had lovely voices, more beautiful than any human being's, and when a storm was coming on, and they thought some ships might be lost, they would swim before the ships and sing most beautifully of how pretty it was at the bottom of the sea, and bade the seafarers not to be afraid of coming down there.

But they could not understand their words; they thought it was the storm. Nor did they see any beautiful things down there either, for when the ship sank they were drowned, and only as dead corpses did they ever reach the sea King's palace.

When of an evening the sisters rose like this, arm in arm, up through the sea, their little sister was left behind quite alone, looking after them, and it seemed as if she must have wept, but a mermaid has no tears, and that makes her suffer all the more.

'Oh! if only I was fifteen,' she said, 'I know I shall become really fond of that world up there and of the people who have their homes there!'

At last she was fifteen years old.

'There now! We've got you off our hands,' said the grandmother, the old widow Queen. 'Come here, and let me dress you out like your other sisters'; and she put a wreath of white lilies on her hair, only every petal in the flower was a half-pearl, and the old lady made eight large oysters take tight hold of the Princess's tail, to indicate her high rank.

'But it hurts so,' said the little mermaid.

'Yes, one must suffer a little for smartness' sake,' said the old lady.

She would gladly have shaken off all this finery and put away the heavy wreath. The red flowers in her garden became her much better; but she dare not change it. 'Good-bye,' she said, and rose bright and light as a bubble, up through the water. The sun had just gone down when she lifted her head above the sea, but all the clouds were still glowing like gold and roses, and in the midst of the pale red heaven the evening star shone.

FAIRY & FOLK TALES

My men are eager,
my men are ready
To drag you below the waves
— Donald Mackenzie

from UNDINE

FRIEDRICH DE LA MOTTE FOUQUÉ

Toward evening Undine was hanging upon the knight's arm with lowly tenderness, while she drew him gently out before the door, where the setting sun shone richly over the fresh grass, and upon the high, slender boles of the trees. Her emotion was visible: the dew of sadness and love swam in her eyes, while a tender and fearful secret seemed to hover upon her lips, but was only made known by hardly-breathed sighs. She led her husband farther and farther onward without speaking. When he asked her questions, she replied only with looks, in which, it is true, there appeared to be no immediate answer to his inquiries, but a whole heaven of love and timid devotion. Thus they reached the margin of the swollen forest stream, and the knight was astonished to see it gliding away with so gentle a murmuring of its waves, that no vestige of its former swell and wildness was now discernible.

'By morning it will be wholly drained off,' said the beautiful wife, almost weeping, 'and you will then be able to travel, without anything to hinder you, whithersoever you will.'

'Not without you, dear Undine,' replied the knight, laughing; 'think, only, were I disposed to leave you, both the Church and the spiritual powers, the Emperor and the laws of the realm, would require the fugitive to be seized and restored to you.'

'All this depends on you – all depends on you,' whispered his little companion, half weeping and half smiling. 'But I still feel sure that you will not leave me; I love you too deeply to fear that misery. Now bear me over to that little island which lies before us. There shall the decision be made. I could easily, indeed, glide through that mere rippling of the water without your aid, but it is so sweet to lie in your arms; and should you determine to put me away, I shall have rested in them once more,... for the last time.'

Huldbrand was so full of strange anxiety and emotion, that he knew not what answer to make her. He took her in his arms and carried her over, now first realizing the fact that this was the same little island from which he had borne her back to the old fisherman, the first night of his arrival. On the farther side, he placed her upon the soft grass, and was throwing himself lovingly near his beautiful burden; but she said to him, 'Not here, but opposite me. I shall read my doom in your eyes, even before your lips pronounce it: now listen attentively to what I shall relate to you.' And she began:

'You must know, my own love, that there are beings in the elements which bear the strongest resemblance to the human race, and which, at the same time, but seldom become visible to you. The wonderful salamanders sparkle and sport amid the flames; deep in the earth the meagre and malicious gnomes pursue their revels; the forest-spirits belong to the air, and wander in the woods; while in the seas, rivers, and streams live the widespread race of water-spirits. These last, beneath resounding domes of crystal, through which the sky can shine with its sun and stars, inhabit a region of light and beauty; lofty coral-trees glow with blue and crimson fruits in their gardens; they walk over the pure sand of the sea, among exquisitely variegated shells, and amid whatever of beauty the old world possessed, such as the present is no more worthy to enjoy – creations which the floods covered with their secret veils of silver; and now these noble monuments sparkle below, stately and solemn, and bedewed by the water, which loves them, and calls forth from their crevices delicate moss-flowers and enwreathing tufts of sedge.

'Now the nation that dwell there are very fair and lovely to behold, for the most part more beautiful than human beings. Many a fisherman has been so fortunate as to catch a view of a delicate maiden of the waters, while she was floating and singing upon the deep. He would then spread far the fame of her beauty; and to such wonderful females men are wont to give the name of Undines. But what need of saying more? – You, my dear husband, now actually behold an Undine before you.'

The knight would have persuaded himself that his lovely wife was under the influence of one of her odd whims, and that she was only amusing herself and him with her extravagant inventions. He wished it might be so. But with whatever emphasis he said this to himself, he still could not credit the hope for a moment: a strange shivering shot through his soul; unable to utter a word, he gazed upon the sweet speaker with a fixed eye. She shook her head in distress, sighed from her full heart, and then proceeded in the following manner: – 'We should be far superior to you, who are another race of the human family, – for we also call ourselves human beings, as we resemble them in form and features – had we not one evil peculiar to ourselves. Both we and the beings I have mentioned as inhabiting the other elements vanish into air at death and go out of existence, spirit and body, so that no vestige of us remains; and when you hereafter awake to a purer state of being, we shall remain where sand, and sparks, and wind, and waves remain. Thus we have no souls; the element moves us, and, again, is obedient to our will, while we live, though it scatters us like dust when we die; and as we have nothing to trouble us, we are as merry as nightingales, little gold-fishes, and other pretty children of nature.

'But all beings aspire to rise in the scale of existence higher than they are. It was therefore the wish of my father, who is a powerful water-prince in the Mediterranean Sea, that his only daughter should become possessed of a soul, although she should have to endure many of the sufferings of those who share that gift.

'Now the race to which I belong have no other means of obtaining a soul than by forming with an individual of your own the most intimate union of love. I am now possessed of a soul, and my soul thanks you, my best beloved, and never shall cease to thank you, if you do not render my whole future life miserable. For what will become of me, if you avoid and reject me? Still, I would not keep you as my own by artifice. And should you decide to cast me off, then do it now, and return alone to the shore. I will plunge into this brook, where my uncle will receive me; my uncle, who here in the forest, far removed from his other friends, passes his strange and solitary existence. But he is powerful, as well as revered and beloved by many great rivers; and as he brought me hither to the fisherman a light-hearted and laughing child, he will take me home to my parents a woman, gifted with a soul, with power to love and to suffer.'

She was about to add something more, when Huldbrand, with the most heartfelt tenderness and love, clasped her in his arms, and again bore her back to the shore. There, amid tears and kisses, he first swore never to forsake his affectionate wife, and esteemed himself even more happy than Pygmalion, for whom Venus gave life to his beautiful statue, and thus changed it into a beloved wife. Supported by his arm, and in the confidence of affection, Undine returned to the cottage; and now she first realized with her whole heart how little cause she had for regretting what she had left – the crystal palace of her mysterious father.

from
FAIRIES ON THE SEA SHORE

LETITIA ELIZABETH LANDON

My palace is in the coral cave
Set with spars by the ocean wave;
Would ye have gems, then seek them there,–
There found I the pearls that bind my hair.
I and the wind together can roam
Over the green waves and their white foam,–
See, I have got this silver shell,
Mark how my breath will its smallness swell,
For the Nautilus is my boat
In which I over the waters float,–
The moon is shining over the sea,
Who is there will come sail with me?

THE GREAT SILKIE OF SULE SKERRY

FRANCIS JAMES CHILD

An earthly nourris sits and sing,
And aye she sings, 'Ba, lily wean!
Little ken I my bairn's father,
Far less the land that he staps in.'

Then ane arose at her bed-fit,
An a grumly guest I'm sure was he:
'Here am I, thy bairn's father,
Although that I be not comelie.

'I am a man, upo the lan,
An I am a silkie in the sea;
And when I'm far and far frae lan,
My dwelling is in Sule Skerrie.'

'It was na weel,' quo the maiden fair,
'It was na weel, indeed,' quo she,
'That the Great Silkie of Sule Skerrie
Suld hae come and aught a bairn to me.'

Now he has taen a purse of goud,
And he has pat it upo her knee,
Sayin, Gie to me my little young son,
An tak thee up thy nourris-fee.

An it sall come to pass on a simmer's day,
When the sin shines het on evera stane,
That I will tak my little young son,
An teach him for to swim the faem.

An thu sall marry a proud gunner,
An a proud gunner I'm sure he'll be,
An the very first schot that ere he schoots,
He'll schoot baith my young son and me.

THE SILKIE WIFE

PATRICK KENNEDY

Those in the Shetland and Orkney Islands who know no better, are persuaded that the seals, or silkies, as they call them, can doff their coverings at times, and disport themselves as men and women.

A fisher once turning a ridge of rock, discovered a beautiful bit of green turf adjoining the shingle, sheltered by rocks on the landward side, and over this turf and shingle two beautiful women chasing each other. Just at the man's feet lay two sealskins, one of which he took up to examine it.

The women, catching sight of him, screamed out, and ran to get possession of the skins. One seized the article on the ground, donned it in a thrice, and plunged into the sea; the other wrung her hands, cried, and begged the fisher to restore her property; but he wanted a wife, and would not throw away the chance. He wooed her so earnestly and lovingly, that she put on some woman's clothing which he brought her from his cottage, followed him home, and became his wife.

Some years later, when their home was enlivened by the presence of two children, the husband, awakening one night, heard voices in conversation from the kitchen. Stealing softly to the room door, he heard his wife talking in a low tone with someone outside the window. The interview was just at an end, and he had only time to ensconce himself in bed, when his wife was stealing across the room. He was greatly disturbed, but determined to do or say nothing till he should acquire further knowledge.

Next evening, as he was returning home by the strand, he spied a male and female phoca sprawling on a rock a few yards out at sea.

The rougher animal, raising himself on his tail and fins, thus addressed the astonished man in the dialect spoken in these islands, 'You deprived me of her whom I was to make my companion; and it was only yesternight that I discovered her outer garment, the loss of which obliged her to be your wife. I bear no malice, as you were kind to her in your own fashion; besides, my heart is too full of joy to hold any malice. Look on your wife for the last time.'

The other seal glanced at him with all the shyness and sorrow she could force into her now uncouth features; but when the bereaved husband rushed toward the rock to secure his lost treasure, she and her companion were in the water on the other side of it in a moment, and the poor fisherman was obliged to return sadly to his motherless children and desolate home.

from
ADDRESS TO THE DEIL

ROBERT BURNS

When thowes dissolve the snawy hoord
An' float the jinglin' icy boord
Then, water-kelpies haunt the foord
By your direction
And 'nighted trav'llers are allur'd
To their destruction.

from
THE KELPIE OF CORRYVRECKAN

CHARLES MACKAY

He mounted his steed of the water clear,
And sat on his saddle of sea-weed sere;
He held his bridal of strings of pearl,
Dug out of the depths where the sea-snakes curl.

He put on his vest of the whirlpool froth,
Soft and dainty as velvet cloth,
And donn'd his mantle of sand so white,
And grasp'd his sword of the coral bright.

And away he gallop'd, a horseman free,
Spurring his steed through the stormy sea,
Clearing the billows with bound and leap —
Away, away, o'er the foaming deep.

By Scarba's rock, by Lunga's shore,
By Garveloch isles where breakers roar,
With his horse's hoofs he dash'd the spray,
And on to Loch Buy, away, away!

On to Loch Buy all day he rode,
And reach'd the shore as sunset glow'd,
And stopp'd to hear the sounds of joy,
That rose from the hills and glens of Moy.

The morrow was May, and on the green
They'd lit the fire of Beltan E'en,
And danced around, and piled it high
With peat and heather, and pine logs dry.

A piper play'd a lightsome reel,
And timed the dance with toe and heel;
While wives look'd on, as lad and lass
Trod it merrily o'er the grass.

And Jessie (fickle and fair was she)
Sat with Evan beneath a tree,
And smiled with mingled love and pride,
And half agreed to be his bride.

The Kelpie gallop'd o'er the green –
He seem'd a knight of noble mien;
And old and young stood up to see,
And wonder'd who the knight could be.

His flowing locks were auburn bright,
His cheeks were ruddy, his eyes flash'd light;
And as he sprang from his good gray steed,
He look'd a gallant youth indeed.

And Jessie's fickle heart beat high,
As she caught the stranger's glancing eye;
And when he smiled, 'Ah well,' thought she,
'I wish this knight came courting me!'

He took two steps towards her seat –
'Wilt thou be mine, O maiden sweet?'
He took her lily-white hand, and sigh'd,
'Maiden, maiden, be my bride!'

And Jessie blush'd, and whisper'd soft –
'Meet me to-night when the moon's aloft.
I've dream'd, fair knight, long time of thee –
I thought thou camest courting me.'

When the moon her yellow horn display'd,
Alone to the trysting went the maid;
When all the stars were shining bright,
Alone to the trysting went the knight.

'I have loved thee long, I have loved thee well,
Maiden, oh more than words can tell!
Maiden, thine eyes like diamonds shine;
Maiden, maiden, be thou mine!'

'Fair sir, thy suit I'll ne'er deny –
Though poor my lot, my hopes are high;
I scorn a lover of low degree –
None but a knight shall marry me.'

He took her by the hand so white,
And gave her a ring of gold so bright;
'Maiden, whose eyes like diamonds shine,
Maiden, maiden, now thou'rt mine!'

He lifted her up on his steed of gray,
And they rode till morning away, away –
Over the mountain and over the moor,
And over the rocks to the dark sea-shore.

'We have ridden east, we have ridden west –
I'm weary, fair knight, and I fain would rest.
Say, is thy dwelling beyond the sea?
Hast thou a good ship waiting for me?'

'I have no dwelling beyond the sea,
I have no good ship waiting for thee:
Thou shalt sleep with me on a couch of foam,
And the depths of the ocean shall be thy home.'

The gray steed plunged in the billows clear,
And the maiden's shrieks were sad to hear; –
'Maiden, whose eyes like diamonds shine –
Maiden, maiden, now thou'rt mine!'

Loud the cold sea-blast did blow
As they sank 'mid the angry waves below –
Down to the rocks where the serpents creep,
Twice five hundred fathoms deep.

At morn a fisherman sailing by
Saw her pale corse floating high.
He knew the maid by her yellow hair
And her lily skin so soft and fair.

Under a rock on Scarba's shore,
Where the wild winds sigh and the breakers roar,
They dug her a grave by the water clear,
Among the sea-weeds salt and sere.

And every year at Beltan E'en,
The Kelpie gallops across the green,
On a steed as fleet as the wintry wind,
With Jessie's mournful ghost behind.

I warn you, maids, whoever you be,
Beware of pride and vanity;
And ere on change of love you reckon,
Beware the Kelpie of Corryvreckan.

from BROWNIES AND BOGLES

LOUISE IMOGEN GUINEY

Of old, there were Oreads and Naiads to people the rivers and the sea, but they were not fairies; and in after-years the beautiful, bright water-life of Greece, with its shells and dolphins, its palaces, its subaqueous music, and its happy-hearted maids and men, faded wholly out of memory. No one dominant race came to replace them. Merpeople, Tritons and Sirens we meet now and then, as did Hendrik Hudson's crew, and the Moruachs of Ireland, the Morverch (sea-daughters) of Brittainy; but they, too, were grown, and half-human. They were beautiful and swift, and usually sat combing their long hair, with a mirror in one hand, and their glossy tails tapering from the waist. The Danish Mermaid was gold-haired, cunning and treacherous; the Havmand or Merman was handsome, too, with black hair and beard, but kind and beneficent.

The Swedish pair offered presents to those on shore, or passing in boats, in hopes to sink them beneath the waves.

England and Ireland had no water-sprites which answered to the Nix and the Kelpie, only the Merrow, who was a Mermaid. She was a fair woman, with white, webbed fingers. She carried upon her head a little diving-cap, and when she came up to the rocks or the beach, she laid it by; but if it were stolen from her, she lost the power of returning to the sea. So that if her cap were taken by a young man, she very often could do nothing better than to marry him, and spend her time hunting for it up and down over his house. And once she had found it, she forgot all else but her desire to go home to 'the kind sea-caves,' and despite the calling of her neighbors and husband and children, she flitted to the shore, and plunged into the first oncoming billow, and walked the earth no longer.

Tales of these spirit-brides who suddenly deserted the green earth for their dear native waters, are common in Arabian and European folk-lore. And this characteristic was noted also in the Sea-trows of the Shetland Islands, who divested themselves of a shining fish-skin, and could not find the way to their ocean-beds if it were kept out of their reach. It was the Danish sailor's belief that seals laid by their skins every ninth night, and took maiden's forms wherewith to sport and sleep on the reefs. And for their capture as they were, warm, living and human, one had only to snatch and hide away their talisman-skin.

The strange German Water-man wore a green hat, and when he opened his mouth, his teeth as well were green; he appeared to girls who passed his lake, and measured out ribbon, and flung it to them.

But we must search for smaller sprites than these.

The little water-fairies who devoted themselves to drawing under whomsoever encroached on their pools and brooks, were called Nixies in Germany, Korrigans (for this was part of their office) in Brittainy; Ondins about Magdebourg, and Roussalkis, the long-haired, smiling ones, among the Slavic people.

The engaging Nixies were very minute and mischievous, and abounded in the Shetland Isles and Cornwall, as did, moreover, the Kelpies, who were like tiny horses, known even in China; sporting on the margin, and foreboding death by drowning, to any who beheld them; or tempting passers-by to mount, and plunging, with their victims, headlong into the deep. The Nix-lady was recognized when she came on shore by the edges of her dress or apron being perpetually wet. The dark-eyed Nix-man with his seaweed hair and his wide hat, was known by his slit ears and feet, which he was very careful to conceal. Once in a while he was observed to be half-fish. The naked Nixen were draped with moss and kelp; but when they were clothed, they seemed merely little men and women, save that the borders of their garments, dripping water, betrayed them. They did their marketing ashore, wheresoever they were, and, according to all accounts, with a sharp eye to economy. Like the land-elves, they loved to dance and sing. Nix did not favor divers, fishermen, and other intruders on his territory, and he did his best to harm them. He was altogether a fierce, grudging, covetous little creature. His comelier wife was much better-natured, and befriended human beings to the utmost of her power.

Near Ghent was a little old Nix who lived in the Scheldt; he cried and sighed much, and did mischief to no one. It grieved him when children ran away from him, yet if they asked what troubled his conscience, he only sighed heavily, and disappeared.

The modern Greeks believed in a black sprite haunting wells and springs, who was fond of beckoning to strangers. If they came to him, he bestowed gifts upon them; if not, he never seemed angry, but turned patiently to wait for the next passer-by.

There was a curious sea-creature in Norway, who swam about as a thin little old man with no head. About the magical Isle of Rügen lived the Nickel. His favorite game was to astonish the fishers, by hauling their boats up among the trees.

At Arles and other towns near the Spanish border in France, were the Dracs, who inhabited clear pools and streams, and floated along in the shape of gold rings and cups, so that women and children bathing should grasp them, and be lured under.

The Indian water-manittos, the Nibanaba, were winning in appearance, and wicked in disposition. They, joining the Pukwudjinies, helped to kill Kwasind.

In Wales were the Gwragedd Annwn, elves who loved the stillness of lonely mountain-lakes, and who seldom ventured into the upper world. They had their own submerged towns and battlements; and from their little sunken city the fairy-bells sent out, ever and anon, muffled silver voices. The Gwragedd Annwn were not fishy-finned, nor were they ever dwellers in the sea; for in Wales were no mermaid-traditions, nor any tales of those who beguiled mortals.

The Neck and the Strömkarl of Swedish rivers were two little chaps with hardly a hair's breadth of difference. Either appeared under various shapes; now as a green-hatted old man with a long beard, out of which he wrung water as he sat on the cliffs; now loitering of a summer night on the surface, like a chip of wood or a leaf, he seemed a fair child, harping, with yellow ringlets falling from beneath a high red cap to his shoulders. Both fairies had a genius for music; and the Strömkarl, especially, had one most marvellous tune to which he put eleven variations. Now, to ten of them any one might dance decorously, and with safety; but at the eleventh, which was the enchanted one, all the world went mad; and tables, belfries, benches, houses, windmills, trees, horses, cripples, babies, ghosts, and whole towns full of sedate citizens began capering on the banks about the invisible player, and kept it up in furious fashion until the last note died away.

You know that the wren was hunted in certain countries on a certain day. Well, here is one legend about her. There was a malicious fairy once in the Isle of Man, very winsome to look at, who worked a sorry Kelpie-trick, on the young men of the town, and inveigled them into the sea, where they perished. At last the inhabitants rose in vengeance, and suspecting her of causing their loss and sorrow, gave her chase so hard and fast by land, that to save herself, she changed her shape into that of an innocent brown wren. And because she had been so treacherous, a spell was cast upon her, inasmuch as she was obliged every New Year's Day to fly about as that same bird, until she should be killed by a human hand. And from sunrise to sunset, therefore, on the first bleak day of January, all the men and boys of the island fired at the poor wrens, and stoned them, and entrapped them, in the hope of reaching the one guilty fairy among them. And as they could never be sure that they had captured the right one, they kept on year by year, chasing and persecuting the whole flock. But every dead wren's feather they preserved carefully, and believed that it hindered them from drowning and shipwreck for that twelvemonth; and they took the feathers with them on voyages great and small, in order that the bad fairy's magic may never be able to prevail, as it had prevailed of yore with their unhappy brothers.

The presence of the sea-fairies had a terror in it, and against their arts only the strongest and most watchful could hope to be victorious. Their sport was to desolate peaceful homes, and bring destruction on gallant ships. They, dwelling in streams and in the ocean, the world over, were like the waters they loved: gracious and noble in aspect, and meaning danger and death to the unwary. We fear that, like the earth-fairies, they were heartless quite.

But it may be that the gentle Nixies had only a blind longing for human society, and would not willingly have wrought harm to the creatures of another element. We are more willing to urge excuses for their wrong-doing than for the like fault in our frowzly under-ground folk; for ugliness seems, somehow, not so shocking when allied with evil as does beauty, which was destined for all men's delight and uplifting. As the air-elves had their Fairyland whither mortal children wandered, and whence they returned after an unmeasured lapse of time, still children, to the ivy-grown ruins of their homes, so the water-elves had a reward for those they snatched from earth; and legends assure us the wave-rocked prisoners a hundred fathoms down, never grew old, but kept the flush of their last morning rosy ever on their brows.

Among a little community full of guile, there is great comfort in spotting one honest, kind water-boy, who, not content with being harmless, as were the Flemish and Grecian Nixies, put himself to work to do good, and charm away some of the worries and ills that burdened the upper world. His name was Hob, and he lived in Hobhole, which was a cave scooped out by the beating tides in old Northumbria.

The lean pockets of the neighboring doctors were partly attributed to this benignant little person; for he set up an opposition, and his specialty was the cure of whooping-cough. Many a Scotch mother took her lad or lass to the spray-covered mouth of the wise goblin's cave, and sang in a low voice:

Hobhole Hob!
Ma bairn's gotten t' kink-cough:
Tak't off! tak't off!

And so he did, sitting there with his toes in the sea. For Hobhole Hob's small sake, we can afford to part friends with the whole naughty race of water-folk.

THE ROUSSALKA

ALEXANDER PUSHKIN

By a lake once in forest darkness
A monk his soul was saving,
Ever in stern occupation
Of prayer, fast, and labor.
Already with slackened shovel
The aged man his grave was digging,
And only for death in peace and quiet
To his saintly patrons prayed he.

Once in summer at the threshold
Of his drooping little hut
To God was praying the hermit.
Darker grew the forest.
Over the lake was rising fog.
And in the clouds the reddish moon
Was gently rolling along the sky.
Upon the waters the hermit gazed.

He looks, and fears, and knows not why,
Himself he cannot understand...
Now he sees: the waves are seething
And suddenly again are quiet...

Suddenly ... as light as shade of night,
As white as early snow of hills,
Out cometh a woman naked
And on the shore herself she seats.

Upon the aged monk she gazes
And she combs her moistened tresses–
The holy monk with terror trembles,
Upon her charms still he gazes;
With her hand to him she beckons
And her head she's quickly nodding....
And suddenly like a falling star
The dreamy wave she vanished under.

The sober monk, all night he slept not,
And all day he prayed not
The shadow unwittingly before him
Of the wondrous maid he ever sees.
Again the forest is clad in darkness,
Along the clouds the moon is sailing.
Again the maid above the water,
Pale and splendent there she sits.

Gaze her eyes, nods her head,
Throws kisses, and she's sporting,
The wave she sprinkles, and she frolics;
Child-like weeping now and laughing;

Sobbing tender – the monk she calls:
Monk, O monk, to me, to me!
Into the waves transparent she dashes;
And again is all in silence deep.

But on the third day the roused hermit
The enchanted shores nigh sitting was,
And the beautiful maid he awaited.
Upon the trees were falling shades...
Night at last by dawn was chased–
And nowhere monk could be found,
His beard alone, the gray one
In the water the boys could see.

from MORNING, ON THE SEA-SHORE

ANN RADCLIFFE

What print of fairy feet is here
On Neptune's smooth and yellow sands?
What midnight revel's airy dance,
Beneath the moon-beam's trembling glance
Has blest these shores? – What sprightly bands
Have chac'd the waves uncheck'd by fear?
Whoe'er they were they fled from morn,
For now, all silent and forlorn,
These tide-forsaken sands appear –
Return, sweet sprites! the scene to cheer!

In vain the call! – 'Till moonlight's hour
Again diffuse its softer pow'r,
Titania, nor her fairy loves,
Emerge from India's spicy groves.
Then, when the shad'wy hour returns,
When silence reigns o'er air and earth,
And ev'ry star in æther burns,
They come to celebrate their mirth;
In frolic ring light trip the ground,
Bid Music's voice on Silence win,
'Till magic echoes answer round –
Thus do their festive rites begin.

O fairy forms so coy to mortal ken,
Your mystic steps to poets only shewn;
O! lead me to the brook, or hollow'd glen,
Retiring far, with winding woods o'ergrown!
Where'er ye best delight to rule;
If in some forest's lone retreat,
Thither conduct my willing feet
To the light brink of fountain cool,
Where, sleeping in the midnight dew,
Lie Spring's young buds of ev'ry hue,
Yielding their sweet breath to the air;
To fold their silken leaves from harm,
And their chill heads in moonshine warm,
Is bright Titania's tender care.

[...]

E'en now your scenes enchanted meet my sight!
I see the earth unclose, the palace rise,
The high dome swell, and long arcades of light
Glitter among the deep embow'ring woods,
And glance reflecting from the trembling floods!
While to soft lutes the portals wide unfold,
And fairy forms, of fine ætherial dyes,
Advance with frolic step and laughing eyes,
Their hair with pearl, their garments deck'd with gold;
Pearls that in Neptune's briny waves they sought,
And gold from India's deepest caverns brought.
Thus your light visions to my eyes unveil,
Ye sportive pleasures, sweet illusion, hail!
But ah! at morn's first blush again ye fade!
So from youth's ardent gaze life's landscape gay,
And forms in Fancy's summer hues array'd,
Dissolve at once in air at Truth's resplendent day!

from
FAIRY AND FOLK TALES OF THE IRISH PEASANTRY

W B YEATS

The *Merrow*, or if you write it in the Irish, Moruadh or Murrúghach, from muir, sea, and oigh, a maid, is not uncommon, they say, on the wilder coasts. The fishermen do not like to see them, for it always means coming gales. The male Merrows (if you can use such a phrase – I have never heard the masculine of Merrow) have green teeth, green hair, pig's eyes, and red noses; but their women are beautiful, for all their fish tails and the little duck-like scale between their fingers. Sometimes they prefer, small blame to them, good-looking fishermen to their sea lovers. Near Bantry, in the last century, there is said to have been a woman covered all over with scales like a fish, who was descended from such a marriage. Sometimes they come out of the sea, and wander about the shore in the shape of little hornless cows. They have, when in their own shape, a red cap, called a cohullen druith, usually covered with feathers. If this is stolen, they cannot again go down under the waves.

NIXIES, NYMPHS & NAIADS

Ne'er did Grecian chisel trace
A Nymph, a Naiad, or a Grace,
Of finer form or lovelier face
— Sir Walter Scott

from
THE ILIAD

HOMER

Then Achilles gave a loud cry and his mother heard him as she was sitting in the depths of the sea by the old man her father, whereon she screamed, and all the goddesses daughters of Nereus that dwelt at the bottom of the sea, came gathering round her. There were Glauce, Thalia and Cymodoce, Nesaia, Speo, Thoe and dark-eyed Halie, Cymothoe, Actaea and Limnorea, Melite, Iaera, Amphithoe and Agave, Doto and Proto, Pherusa and Dynamene, Dexamene, Amphinome and Callianeira, Doris, Panope, and the famous sea-nymph Galatea, Nemertes, Apseudes and Callianassa. There were also Clymene, Ianeira and Ianassa, Maera, Oreithuia and Amatheia of the lovely locks, with other Nereids who dwell in the depths of the sea. The crystal cave was filled with their multitude and they all beat their breasts while Thetis led them in their lament.

'Listen,' she cried, 'sisters, daughters of Nereus, that you may hear the burden of my sorrows. Alas, woe is me, woe in that I have borne the most glorious of offspring. I bore him fair and strong, hero among heroes, and he shot up as a sapling; I tended him as a plant in a goodly garden, and sent him with his ships to Ilius to fight the Trojans, but never shall I welcome him back to the house of Peleus. So long as he lives to look upon the light of the sun he is in heaviness, and though I go to him I cannot help him. Nevertheless I will go, that I may see my dear son and learn what sorrow has befallen him though he is still holding aloof from battle.'

She left the cave as she spoke, while the others followed weeping after, and the waves opened a path before them. When they reached the rich plain of Troy, they came up out of the sea in a long line on to the sands, at the place where the ships of the Myrmidons were drawn up in close order round the tents of Achilles. His mother went up to him as he lay groaning; she laid her hand upon his head and spoke piteously, saying, 'My son, why are you thus weeping? What sorrow has now befallen you? Tell me; hide it not from me. Surely Jove has granted you the prayer you made him, when you lifted up your hands and besought him that the Achaeans might all of them be pent up at their ships, and rue it bitterly in that you were no longer with them.'

Achilles groaned and answered, 'Mother, Olympian Jove has indeed vouchsafed me the fulfilment of my prayer, but what boots it to me, seeing that my dear comrade Patroclus has fallen – he whom I valued more than all others, and loved as dearly as my own life? I have lost him; aye, and Hector when he had killed him stripped the wondrous armour, so glorious to behold, which the gods gave to Peleus when they laid you in the couch of a mortal man. Would that you were still dwelling among the immortal sea-nymphs, and that Peleus had taken to himself some mortal bride. For now you shall have grief infinite by reason of the death of that son whom you can never welcome home – nay, I will not live nor go about among mankind unless Hector fall by my spear, and thus pay me for having slain Patroclus son of Menoetius.'

Thetis wept and answered, 'Then, my son, is your end near at hand – for your own death awaits you full soon after that of Hector.'

Then said Achilles in his great grief, 'I would die here and now, in that I could not save my comrade. He has fallen far from home, and in his hour of need my hand was not there to help him. What is there for me? Return to my own land I shall not, and I have brought no saving neither to Patroclus nor to my other comrades of whom so many have been slain by mighty Hector; I stay here by my ships a bootless burden upon the earth, I, who in fight have no peer among the Achaeans, though in council there are better than I. Therefore, perish strife both from among gods and men, and anger, wherein even a righteous man will harden his heart – which rises up in the soul of a man like smoke, and the taste thereof is sweeter than drops of honey. Even so has Agamemnon angered me. And yet – so be it, for it is over; I will force my soul into subjection as I needs must; I will go; I will pursue Hector who has slain him whom I loved so dearly, and will then abide my doom when it may please Jove and the other gods to send it. Even Hercules, the best beloved of Jove – even he could not escape the hand of death, but fate and Juno's fierce anger laid him low, as I too shall lie when I am dead if a like doom awaits me. Till then I will win fame, and will bid Trojan and Dardanian women wring tears from their tender cheeks with both their hands in the grievousness of their great sorrow; thus shall they know that he who has held aloof so long will hold aloof no longer. Hold me not back, therefore, in the love you bear me, for you shall not move me.'

Then silver-footed Thetis answered, 'My son, what you have said is true. It is well to save your comrades from destruction, but your armour is in the hands of the Trojans; Hector bears it in triumph upon his own shoulders. Full well I know that his vaunt shall not be lasting, for his end is close at hand; go not, however, into the press of battle till you see me return hither; to-morrow at break of day I shall be here, and will bring you goodly armour from King Vulcan.'

On this she left her brave son, and as she turned away she said to the sea-nymphs her sisters, 'Dive into the bosom of the sea and go to the house of the old sea-god my father. Tell him everything; as for me, I will go to the cunning workman Vulcan on high Olympus, and ask him to provide my son with a suit of splendid armour.'

When she had so said, they dived forthwith beneath the waves, while silver-footed Thetis went her way that she might bring the armour for her son.

Thus, then, did her feet bear the goddess to Olympus, and meanwhile the Achaeans were flying with loud cries before murderous Hector till they reached the ships and the Hellespont, and they could not draw the body of Mars's servant Patroclus out of reach of the weapons that were showered upon him, for Hector son of Priam with his host and horsemen had again caught up to him like the flame of a fiery furnace; thrice did brave Hector seize him by the feet, striving with might and main to draw him away and calling loudly on the Trojans, and thrice did the two Ajaxes, clothed in valour as with a garment, beat him from off the body; but all undaunted he would now charge into the thick of the fight, and now again he would stand still and cry aloud, but he would give no ground. As upland shepherds that cannot chase some famished lion from a carcase, even so could not the two Ajaxes scare Hector son of Priam from the body of Patroclus.

And now he would even have dragged it off and have won imperishable glory, had not Iris fleet as the wind, winged her way as messenger from Olympus to the son of Peleus and bidden him arm. She came secretly without the knowledge of Jove and of the other gods, for Juno sent her, and when she had got close to him she said, 'Up, son of Peleus, mightiest of all mankind; rescue Patroclus about whom this fearful fight is now raging by the ships. Men are killing one another, the Danaans in defence of the dead body, while the Trojans are trying to hale it away, and take it to wind Ilius: Hector is the most furious of them all; he is for cutting the head from the body and fixing it on the stakes of the wall. Up, then, and bide here no longer; shrink from the thought that Patroclus may become meat for the dogs of Troy. Shame on you, should his body suffer any kind of outrage.'

And Achilles said, 'Iris, which of the gods was it that sent you to me?'

Iris answered, 'It was Juno the royal spouse of Jove, but the son of Saturn does not know of my coming, nor yet does any other of the immortals who dwell on the snowy summits of Olympus.'

Then fleet Achilles answered her saying, 'How can I go up into the battle? They have my armour. My mother forbade me to arm till I should see her come, for she promised to bring me goodly armour from Vulcan; I know no man whose arms I can put on, save only the shield of Ajax son of Telamon, and he surely must be fighting in the front rank and wielding his spear about the body of dead Patroclus.'

Iris said, 'We know that your armour has been taken, but go as you are; go to the deep trench and show yourelf before the Trojans, that they may fear you and cease fighting. Thus will the fainting sons of the Achaeans gain some brief breathing-time, which in battle may hardly be.'

Iris left him when she had so spoken. But Achilles dear to Jove arose, and Minerva flung her tasselled aegis round his strong shoulders; she crowned his head with a halo of golden cloud from which she kindled a glow of gleaming fire. As the smoke that goes up into heaven from some city that is being beleaguered on an island far out at sea – all day long do men sally from the city and fight their hardest, and at the going down of the sun the line of beacon-fires blazes forth, flaring high for those that dwell near them to behold, if so be that they may come with their ships and succour them – even so did the light flare from the head of Achilles, as he stood by the trench, going beyond the wall – but he did not join the Achaeans for he heeded the charge which his mother laid upon him.

from
ENDYMION

JOHN KEATS

They stood in dreams
Till Triton blew his horn. The palace rang;
The Nereids danc'd; the Syrens faintly sang;
And the great Sea-King bow'd his dripping head.
Then Love took wing, and from his pinions shed
On all the multitude a nectarous dew.
The ooze-born Goddess beckoned and drew
Fair Scylla and her guides to conference;
And when they reach'd the throned eminence
She kist the sea-nymph's cheek

THE NEREID

ANNE BANNERMAN

Deep in thy ruby-colour'd cave,
Hear, Nereid of the sacred main!
And, from the Ocean's stormy wave,
To these fair fields return again.
Blows there among thy emerald bowers
A gale like this, that, fluttering still,
Attendant on the month of flowers,
Breathes on this green and sunny hill ?

What tho' along thy foamy verge
The Halcyon skims her downy breast;
And, cradled on the murmuring surge
The west-wind rocks her sea-weed nest:
Thou hear'st not in thy crystal cell
The morning anthem of the year;
The music of thy spiral shell,
The wild waves deafen, sobbing drear!

O to these bowers, the bowers of Spring,
The shades of Nature, holy gloom!
While Heaven's soft dews at twilight fling
On grass and flower their living bloom,
Climena, from thy pearly caves
Return, and hail the Sun of day,
Nor for the roar of tossing waves
Resign the music of the May.

from COMUS

JOHN MILTON

There is a gentle Nymph not farr from hence,
That with moist curb sways the smooth Severn stream,
Sabrina is her name, a Virgin pure,
Whilom she was the daughter of Locrine,
That had the Scepter from his father Brute.
The guiltless damsell flying the mad pursuit
Of her enraged stepdam Guendolen,
Commended her innocence to the flood
That stay'd her flight with his cross-flowing course,
The water Nymphs that in the bottom plaid,
Held up their pearled wrists and took her in,
Bearing her straight to aged Nereus Hall,
Who piteous of her woes, rear'd her lank head,
And gave her to his daughters to imbathe
In nectar'd lavers strew'd with Asphodil,
And through the porch and inlet of each sense
Dropt in Ambrosial Oils till she reviv'd,
And underwent a quick immortal change
Made Goddess of the River; still she retains
Her maid'n gentlenes, and oft at Eeve
Visits the herds along the twilight meadows,
Helping all urchin blasts, and ill luck signes
That the shrewd medling Elf delights to make,
Which she with pretious viold liquors heals.

For which the Shepherds at their festivals
Carrol her goodnes loud in rustick layes,
And throw sweet garland wreaths into her stream
Of pancies, pinks, and gaudy Daffadils.
And, as the old Swain said, she can unlock
The clasping charm, and thaw the numming spell,
If she be right invok't in warbled Song,
For maid'nhood she loves, and will be swift
To aid a Virgin, such as was her self
In hard besetting need, this will I try
And adde the power of som adjuring verse.

Song:
Sabrina fair
Listen where thou art sitting
Under the glassie, cool, translucent wave,
In twisted braids of Lillies knitting
The loose train of thy amber-dropping hair,
Listen for dear honours sake,
Goddess of the silver lake,
Listen and save.

THE WATER-SPRITE

ALIX EGERTON

Nixie, Nixie, in the stream
Why do you hide your face by day?
Are you asleep? And do you dream?
Or do you hide your face in play?

Nixie, Nixie, you may hide
But I can see you over there,
Though into shadowy pools you glide
There floats behind your long green hair.

Nixie, Nixie, sweet and clear
You laugh beneath the water's edge,
It ripples so, and I can hear
Your sighs among the river sedge.

Nixie, Nixie, if at night
I come when all the world's asleep,
Oh, will you hold my hand quite tight
And let me in your palace peep.

Nixie, Nixie, turn your head,
I want to see your laughing eyes;
'There are no Water Sprites,' they said,
But I am a child and I am wise.

from THE RHINEGOLD

RICHARD WAGNER

Alberich: What is it, sleek ones,
That yonder gleams and shines?

The Three Rhine-Maidens: Where dost thou hail from, O churl,
Of the Rhinegold not to have heard?

Wellgunde: Knows not the elf
Of the famed eye golden
That wakes and sleeps in turn?

Woglinde: Of the star resplendent
Down in the depths
Whose light illuminates the waves?

The Three Rhine-Maidens: See how gaily
We glide in the glory!
Wouldst thou also
Be bathed in brightness
Come, float and frolic with us!
Wallala la la leia lalei!
Wallala la la leia jahei!

THE LORELEI

MARK TWAIN

I cannot divine what it meaneth,
This haunting nameless pain:
A tale of the bygone ages
Keeps brooding through my brain:

The faint air cools in the glooming,
And peaceful flows the Rhine,
The thirsty summits are drinking
The sunset's flooding wine;

The loveliest maiden is sitting
High-throned in yon blue air,
Her golden jewels are shining,
She combs her golden hair;

She combs with a comb that is golden,
And sings a weird refrain
That steeps in a deadly enchantment
The list'ner's ravished brain:

The doomed in his drifting shallop,
Is tranced with the sad sweet tone,
He sees not the yawning breakers,
He sees but the maid alone:

The pitiless billows engulf him!–
So perish sailor and bark;
And this, with her baleful singing,
Is the Lorelei's gruesome work.

OVERHEARD ON A SALTMARSH

HAROLD EDWARD MONRO

Nymph, nymph, what are your beads?

Green glass, goblin. Why do you stare at them?

Give them me.
No.

Give them me. Give them me.
No.

Then I will howl all night in the reeds,
Lie in the mud and howl for them.

Goblin, why do you love them so?

They are better than stars or water,
Better than voices of winds that sing,
Better than any man's fair daughter,
Your green glass beads on a silver ring.

Hush, I stole them out of the moon.

Give me your beads, I want them.
No.

I will howl in a deep lagoon
For your green glass beads, I love them so.
Give them me. Give them.
No.

from METAMORPHOSES

OVID

Deep in the sheltering caves of Ida's hill,
The Naiäd nymphs a beauteous infant nurs'd;
Whom Cyprus' goddess unto Hermes bore.
His father's beauty, and his mother's, shone
In every feature; in his name conjoin'd
He bore their appellations. When matur'd
By fifteen summers, from paternal hills
Straying, he wander'd from his nursing Idé:
In lands unknown he joy'd, and joy'd to see
Strange rivers, – pleasure lessening every toil.
Through Lycia's towns he stray'd; and further still,
To bordering Caria, where a pool he spy'd,
Whose lowest depth a gleam transparent shew'd:
No marshy canes, – no filthy barren weeds,
Nor pointed bulrush near the margin grew:
Full on the eye the water shone, yet round
Its brink a border smil'd of verdant turf,
And plants forever green. Here dwelt a nymph,
But one who never join'd the active chace;
The bow who never bent; who never strove
To conquer in the race: of all the nymphs,
Alone no comrade of Diana fleet.
Oft, as 'tis said, her sister-nymphs exclaim'd;–
Come, Salmacis, thy painted quiver take;
Or take thy javelin; – with soft pleasures mix
Laborious sporting: but nor javelin she,
Nor painted quiver took; – with sportive toil,
Soft pleasures mingling: sole intent to bathe,

Her beauteous limbs amidst her own clear waves;
And through her flowing tresses oft to draw
The boxen comb, while o'er the fountain bent,
She studies all her graces: now, her form
Clad in a robe transparent, stretcht she lies,
Or on the yielding leaves, or bending grass;
Now flowers she culls;—and so it chanc'd to fall,
Flowers she was gathering, when she first beheld
The charming youth; no sooner seen than lov'd.
Not forth she rush'd at first, though strongly urg'd,
Forward to spring, but all adjusted fair:
Closely survey'd her robe; her features form'd;
And every part in beauteous shape compos'd.
Then thus address'd him; – O, most godlike youth!
And if a god, the lovely Cupid sure!
But if of mortal mould, blest is thy sire!
Blest is thy brother! and thy sister blest!–
If sister hast thou; – and the fostering breast
Which fed thy infant growth: but far 'bove all
In rapturous bliss, is she who calls thee spouse;
Should nymph exist thou deem'st that bliss deserves!
If wedded, grant a stol'n embrace to me;
If not, let me thy nuptial couch ascend.
The Naiäd ceas'd: a bashful glow suffus'd
His face, for nought of love to him was known:
Yet blushing seem'd he lovely: thus warm glows
The apple, to the ripening sun expos'd;
Or teinted ivory; or the redden'd moon,
Whom brazen cymbals clash to help in vain.
To her, warm praying for at least a kiss,
A chaste, a sister's kiss, – her arms firm claspt
Around his ivory neck; – desist! he cries,
Desist! or sole to thee the place I'll leave.
His flight she dreaded, and reply'd, – I go,
Dear youth, and freely yield the spot to thee.

And seems indeed, her steps from him to turn;
But still in sight she kept him; lurking close
Shelter'd by shadowy shrubs, on bended knees.
Of spy unconscious, he in boyish play
Frisks sportive here and there; dips first his feet,
Then ancles deeper in the wantoning waves;
Pleas'd with the temper of the lucid pool:
Till hasty stript from off his tender limbs
His garments soft he flings. More deeply struck
Stood Salmacis; more fiercely flam'd her love,
His naked beauty seen. Her gloating eyes
Sparkled no less than seem bright Phœbus' rays,
When shining splendid, midst a cloudless sky,
A mirror's face reflecting gives them back.
Delay ill brooking, hardly she contains
Her swelling joy; frantic for his embrace,
She pants, and hard from rushing forth refrains.
His sides he claps, and agile in the steam
Quick plunges, moving with alternate arms.
Bright through the waves he shines; thus white appears
The sculptur'd ivory, or the lily fair,
Seen through a crystal veil. The Naiäd cries;–
Lo! here I come; – he's mine, – the youth's my own!
And instant far was every garment flung.
Midst of the waves she leaps; – the struggling youth
Clasps close; and on his cold reluctant lips,
Forces her kisses; down she girds his arms;
And close to hers hugs his unwilling breast:
Final, around the youth who arduous strives
In opposition, and escape essays,
Her limbs she twines: so twines a serpent huge,
Seiz'd by the bird of Jove, and borne on high,
Twisting his head, the feet close-bracing holds;
The wide-spread wings entangled with his tail:
So twines the ivy round the lengthen'd bough:

So numerous Polypus his foe confines,
Seiz'd in the deep, with claws on every side
Firm graspt. But Hermes' son persisting still,
The Naiäd's wish denies; she presses close,
And as she cleaves, their every limb close join'd
Exclaims; – ungallant boy! but strive thy most,
Thou shalt not fly me. Grant me, O ye gods!
No time may ever sunder him from me,
Or me from him. – Her prayer was granted straight;–
For now, commingling, both their bodies join'd;
And both their faces melted into one.
So, when in growth we boughs ingrafted see,
The bark inclosing both at once, they sprout.
Thus were their limbs, in strong embrace comprest,
Wrapp'd close; no longer two in form, yet two
In feature; nor a nymph-like face remain'd,
Nor yet a boy's: it both and neither seem'd.

When Hermes' son beheld the liquid stream,
Where masculine he plung'd, the power possess
To enervate his body, and his limbs
Effeminately soften; high he rais'd
His arms, and pray'd (but not with manly voice)
O, sire! O, mother dear! indulge your son,
Your double appellation bearing, this
Sole-urg'd petition. Whoso in these waves
In strong virility, like me, shall plunge,
Hence let him go, like me enervate made;
Spoilt by the stream his strength. Each parent god
Nodding, confirm'd their alter'd son's request;
And ting'd the fountain with the changing power.

THE NYMPH OF LAKE SWITEZ

ADAM MICKIEWICZ

O who is he – so handsome, young and smiling?
And who is she – so beautiful and gay?
They wander in the moonlight round Lake Świteź,
And like a dream the fond hours glide away.

She, smiling, gives him raspberries from her basket;
His gift, as sweet, the flowers in her hair:
Surely he is her true, accepted lover?
And she his dear betrothed, as fond as fair?...

And every night, their hour of bliss returning,
They meet, in rapture, 'neath the larches green:
He is a hunter of the forest round them...
But where she dwelleth none have heard or seen!

So sudden and capricious are her movements
And her strange shapes, – she mocks our search or sight:
She rises from the lake – a water-lily!
And as a will-o'the-wisp escapes at night!

'O tell me, O my sweet and lovely maiden!
Why dost thou let these mysteries grieve me so?
Where is thy home or haunt? and who thy parents?
Why, when day comes, dost thou leave me in woe?

'Summer has gone, and Autumn leaves are yellow,
And Winter soon will come with flood and storm.
O shall I always seek thee by Lake Świteź?
And find thee in thy lovely, fairy form?

'Why dost thou always wander through the forest,
Now as a ghost, now as a shy gazelle?
'Tis better to remain with him who loves thee,
O maiden, stay with me! – I love thee well.

'O stay! – for in these woods I have a cottage,
In a dear hazel-nut wood all my own;
And I have other fruit – and milk – in plenty,
And game the finest that our land has known'.

–'Cease, cease, rash youth! to offer me temptation;
For once my aged father said to me:–
"Men's tongues, my dear! than nightingales are sweeter,
But in their hearts there is vile treachery".

–'I fear thy flatteries and "honied nothings"
More than I trust thy promises of bliss:
If trusted, – thou wouldst prove a gay deceiver,
And, Judas-like, betray me with a kiss.–'

The youth has sworn by all the powers infernal
His love for her is lasting, true and deep;
And then he swears by the bright moon as witness:
Ah! but his oath so fearful will he keep?

–'O hearken to me, hunter!' cries the maiden.
–'And mark my words – the warning words I say:–
He who swears false; – ill to him! – here! – here-after!
And never shall he see Eternal Day!–'

And saying this, the maiden leaves her lover,
Placing his garland on her shapely head;
She will not stay for all his tender pleading,
But runs to her accustomed fields instead.

So rapid are her airy, fairy footsteps
That the poor hunter chases her in vain;
Lo! she has vanished from him like a zephyr,
And he is left in solitude again.

He is alone! – by the wild trail returning
Alone! – without her he would make his bride;–
Forsook! – in twofold night! – and dreadful silence! –
And in a bog!... He would that he had died!

Still some hope lingers: he regains Lake Świteź
And seeks for her so anxiously around;
Sudden the wind moans through the virgin forest,
The water roars! – he startles at the sound.

It heaves, roars, rages – riven to the bottom!
And then out of the depths – O peerless sight!
Above the silvery abyss of Świteź
A lovely maiden beautifies the night!

Like a white rose steeped in the dew of morning,
Her little face so round and bright and fair;
And like a film of mist her veil-robe foldeth
Her dainty limbs and heavenly shape so rare.

–'O youth so full of beauty! O young lover!–'
Said the fair maiden in her silvery tone;
–'For whom around the moonlit Lake of Świteź
Seek'st thou so mournful – making saddest moan?

–'O why lament for one so vain and heartless,
Who, having lured thee here – to my domain,–
Now leaves thee lonely in the lonely forest,
And doubtless laughs at all thy grief and pain?

–'O come to me! quit sighing and quit sorrow,
And be thou sweetly led by words of love;
So come, come to me here! – we'll dance together
On crystal waters, or in the air above.

–'Or, light of heart and wing, be thou a swallow
Skimming the surface in thy pretty play;
Or, nimble as a roach, dart through the water
With me – thy little wife, the nymph – all day:

–'And then at night; – a liquid couch of silver!
The rapture through our crystal tent to peep!
And on the soft, white, fragrant water-lilies,
The bliss of Heaven will mingle with our sleep!–'

Thus ended her sweet music; and as sweetly
From her veil-robe flashes a swan-white breast;
The maiden glides towards the youth and murmurs,–
'O come with me and share my crystal rest'...

Then, leaping in the air with feet allying,
She makes a rainbow-arch against the sky;
And swift rejoining her beloved water
She scatters it in brilliant drops so high.

The hunter runs to leap!... and stops as sudden!
Now he is brave... and now he is not brave...
Till from across the calm and moonlit waters
Falls softly at his feet – an azure wave!

And now she runs off smiling, now caresses,
And who such pretty pleading may withstand?
As when a chaste and sweetly-loving maiden
Secretly presses her dear lover's hand.

The hunter has forgotten his betrothëd,
And he has broken his betrothal vow,
And, charmed by the new allurement, straight is hurled
Headlong into destruction, – even now

He's carried down! down! through a world of waters,
Already he has left the light of day,
And, in the still and silvery depths of Świteź,
Sports where the water-nymphs in secret play;

And now his hand is pressed by snowy fingers,
And lovely features meet his tender gaze,
And his fond lip kisses a lip of coral,
And sweet they dance along enchanting ways.

Sudden! – a whirlwind whistles through the forest
And a dark cloud is emptied of its rain.
Gone his illusion, and he recognises
(Standing beside him) his betrothed again!

–'What of thy solemn oath, O perjured lover?
Hast thou forgot the words I said – and say?–
'He who swears false; ill to him! – here! – here-after!
And never shall he see Eternal Day!'

–'O not for thee! to roam through moonlit waters,
Not for the sinner – Crystal Paradise:
The frozen earth shall soon devour thy body
And sharp flints pierce thy falsely-smiling eyes;

–'And then thy soul beside this Tree of Knowledge
Must grieve in penance for a thousand years,
Suffering ceaseless fire and pangs infernal,
Nor shalt thou slake thy thirst – except with tears!'

The youth, all paralysed by a doom so dreadful,
Attempts not flight, but casts wild glances round;
Again the wind moans through the virgin forest,
The water roars! – he startles at the sound;

It heaves, roars, rages,–riven to the bottom–
And the fierce torrent snatches him away,
And the abyss opens wide jaws and swallows
Both him and the young maiden as its prey!

Ages have passed... and still the Lake forms bubbles;
Still, on a moonlight night, you will discover
Two wand'ring shades, which, as tradition tells us,
Are those of the young maiden and her lover.

She glides, in silence, o'er the silver'd billow,
And he, beneath this oak-tree, groans in woe.
Who is the youth? – a hunter of the forest,
And the young maiden? – ah! I do not know.

THE SEA-NYMPH

ANN RADCLIFFE

Down, down a thousand fathom deep,
Among the sounding seas I go;
Play round the foot of every steep
Whose cliffs above the ocean grow.

There, within their secret caves,
I hear the mighty rivers roar;
And guide their streams through Neptune's waves
To bless the green earth's inmost shore:

And bid the freshen'd waters glide,
For fern-crown'd nymphs of lake, or brook,
Through winding woods and pastures wide,
And many a wild, romantic nook.

For this the nymphs, at fall of eve,
Oft dance upon the flow'ry banks,
And sing my name, and garlands weave
To bear beneath the wave their thanks.

In coral bow'rs I love to lie,
And hear the surges roll above,
And, through the waters, view on high
The proud ships sail, and gay clouds move.

And oft at midnight's stillest hour,
When summer seas the vessel lave,
I love to prove my charmful pow'r
While floating on the moon-light wave.

And when deep sleep the crew has bound,
And the sad lover musing leans
O'er the ship's side, I breathe around
Such strains as speak no mortal means!

O'er the dim waves his searching eye
Sees but the vessel's lengthen'd shade;
Above – the moon and azure sky;
Entranc'd he hears, and half afraid!

Sometimes a single note I swell,
That, softly sweet, at distance dies;
Then wake the magic of my shell,
And choral voices round me rise!

The trembling youth, charm'd by my strain,
Calls up the crew, who, silent, bend
O'er the high deck, but list in vain;
My song is hush'd, my wonders end!

Within the mountain's woody bay,
Where the tall bark at anchor rides,
At twilight hour, with tritons gay,
I dance upon the lapsing tides.

And with my sister-nymphs I sport,
'Till the broad sun looks o'er the floods;
Then, swift we seek our crystal court,
Deep in the wave, 'mid Neptune's woods.

In cool arcades and glassy halls
We pass the sultry hours of noon,
Beyond wherever sun-beam falls,
Weaving sea-flowers in gay festoon.

The while we chant our ditties sweet
To some soft shell that warbles near;
Join'd by the murmuring currents, fleet,
That glide along our halls so clear.

There, the pale pearl and sapphire blue,
And ruby red, and em'rald green,
Dart from the domes a changing hue,
And sparry columns deck the scene.

When the dark storm scowls o'er the deep,
And long, long peals of thunder sound,
On some high cliff my watch I keep
O'er all the restless seas around:

'Till on the ridgy wave, afar,
Comes the lone vessel, labouring slow,
Spreading the white foam in the air,
With sail and topmast bending low.

Then, plunge I 'mid the ocean's roar,
My way by quiv'ring lightnings shewn,
To guide the bark to peaceful shore,
And hush the sailor's fearful groan.

And if too late I reach its side
To save it from the 'whelming surge,
I call my dolphins o'er the tide,
To bear the crew where isles emerge.

Their mournful spirits soon I cheer,
While round the desert coast I go,
With warbled songs they faintly hear,
Oft as the stormy gust sinks low.

My music leads to lofty groves,
That wild upon the sea-bank wave;
Where sweet fruits bloom, and fresh spring roves,
And closing boughs the tempest brave.

The spirits of the air obey
My potent voice they love so well;
And, on the clouds, paint visions gay,
While strains more sweet at distance swell.

And thus the lonely hours I cheat,
Soothing the ship-wreck'd sailor's heart,
'Till from the waves the storms retreat,
And o'er the east the day-beams dart.

Neptune for this oft binds me fast
To rocks below, with coral chain,
'Till all the tempest's over-past,
And drowning seamen cry in vain.

Whoe'er ye are that love my lay,
Come, when red sun-set tints the wave,
To the still sands, where fairies play;
There, in cool seas, I love to lave.

ODE TO A WATER NYMPH

WILLIAM MASON

Ye green-hair'd Nymphs! whom Pan's decrees
Have given to guard this sweetly-solemn wood,
To speed the shooting scions into trees,
And call the roseate blossom from the bud,
Attend. But chief, thou Naiad, wont to lead
This fluid crystal sparkling as it flows;
Whither, ah, whither art thou fled?
What shade is conscious to thy woes?
Ah! 'tis yon poplar's awful gloom:
Poetic eyes can pierce the scene;
Can see thy dropping head, thy with'ring bloom;
See grief diffused o'er all thy languid mien.
Well may'st thou wear misfortune's fainting air,
Well rend those flow'ry honours from thy brow;
Devolve that length of careless hair;
And give thine azure veil to flow

Loose to the wind: for, oh, thy pain
The pitying Muse can well relate:
That pitying Muse shall breate her tend'rest strain,
To teach the Echoes thy disastrous fate.
'Twas, where yon beeches' crowding branches closed,
What time the dog-star's fires intensely burn,
In gentlest indolence composed,
Reclined upom thy trickling urn
Slumb'ring thou lay'st, all free from fears;
No friendly dream foretold thine harm,
When sudden, see, the tyrant Art appears,
To snatch the liquid treasures from thy arm.
Art, Gothick Art, has seiz'd thy darling vase:
That vase which silver-slipper'd Thetis gave,
For some soft story told with grace,
Among the associates of the wave;
When in sequester'd coral vales,
While worlds of waters roll'd above,
The circling sea-nymphs told alternate tales
Of fabled changes, and of slighted love.
Ah! loss too justly mourn'd: for now the fiend
Has on yon shell-wrought terras pois'd it high;
And thence he bids its streams descend,
With torturing regularity.
From step to step with sullen sound
The forc'd cascades indignant leap;
Now sinking fill the bason's measur'd round;
There in a dull stagnation doom'd to sleep.
Lost is the vocal pebble's gurgling song?
The rill slow-dripping from its rocky spring?
What free meander winds along,
Or curls, when Zephyr waves his wing?
Alas, these glories are now no more:
Fortune, oh, give me to redeem
The ravish'd vase; oh, give me to restore

Its ancient honours to this hapless stream.
Then, Nymph, again, with all their wonted ease,
Thy wanton waters, volatile and free,
Shall wildly warble, as they please,
Their soft, loquacious harmony.
Where Thou and Nature bid them rove,
There I will gently aid their way;
Whether to darked in the shadowy grove,
Or, in the mead, reflect the dancing ray.
For thee too, Goddess, o'er that hallow's spot,
Where first thy fount of chrystal bubbles bright,
These hands shall arch a rustic grot,
Impervious to the garish light.
I'll not demand of Ocean's pride
To bring his coral spoils from far:
Nor will I delve yon yawning mountain's side,
For latent minerals rough, or polish'd spar:
But antique roots, with ivy dark o'ergrown,
Steep'd in the bosom of the chilly lake,
Thy touch shall turn to living stone;
And these the simple roof shall deck.
Yet grant one melancholy boon:
Grant that, at evening's sober hour,
Led by the lustre of the rising moon,
My step may frequent tread thy pebbled floor.
There, if perchance I wake the love lorn theme,
In melting accents querulously slow,
Kind Naiad, let thy pitying stream
With wailing notes accordant flow:
So shalt thou sooth this heaving heart,
That mourns a faithful virgin lost;
So shall thy murmurs, and my sights impart
Some share of pensive pleasure to her ghost.

from THE FAIRY OF THE FOUNTAINS

LETITIA ELIZABETH LANDON

With a cautious step he steals
To the cave that light reveals.
'Tis such grotto as might be,
Nereïd's home beneath the sea.
Crested with the small bright stars
Of a thousand rainbow spars.
And a fountain from the side
Pours beneath its crystal tide,
In a white and marble bath
Singing on its silvery path;
While a meteor's emerald rays
O'er the lucid water plays.–
Close beside, with wild flowers laid,
Is a couch of green moss made.
There he sees his lady lie;
Pain is in her languid eye,
And amid her hair the dew
Half obscures its golden hue;

Damp and heavy, and unbound,
Its wan clusters sweep around.
On her small hand leans her head,–
See the fevered cheek is red,
And the fiery colour rushes
To her brow in hectic blushes.–
What strange vigil is she keeping!
He can hear that she is weeping.–

He will fling him at her feet,
He will kiss away her tears.
Ah, what doth his wild eyes meet,
What below that form appears?
Downwards from that slender waist,
By a golden zone embraced,
Do the many folds escape,
Of the subtle serpent's shape.–
Bright with many-coloured dyes
All the glittering scales arise,

With a red and purple glow
Colouring the waves below!
At the strange and fearful sight,
Stands in mute despair the knight,–
Soon to feel a worse despair,
Melusina sees him there!
And to see him is to part
With the idol of her heart,
Part as just the setting sun
Tells the fatal day is done.
Vanish all those serpent rings,
To her feet the lady springs,
And the shriek rings through the cell,
Of despairing love's farewell,–
Hope and happiness are o'er,
They can meet on earth no more.

from LE MORTE D'ARTHUR

THOMAS MALORY

And as they rode, Arthur said, I have no sword. No force, said Merlin, hereby is a sword that shall be yours, an I may. So they rode till they came to a lake, the which was a fair water and broad, and in the midst of the lake Arthur was ware of an arm clothed in white samite, that held a fair sword in that hand. Lo! said Merlin, yonder is that sword that I spake of. With that they saw a damosel going upon the lake. What damosel is that? said Arthur. That is the Lady of the Lake, said Merlin; and within that lake is a rock, and therein is as fair a place as any on earth, and richly beseen; and this damosel will come to you anon, and then speak ye fair to her that she will give you that sword. Anon withal came the damosel unto Arthur, and saluted him, and he her again. Damosel, said Arthur, what sword is that, that yonder the arm holdeth above the water? I would it were mine, for I have no sword. Sir Arthur, king, said the damosel, that sword is mine, and if ye will give me a gift when I ask it you, ye shall have it. By my faith, said Arthur, I will give you what gift ye will ask. Well! said the damosel, go ye into yonder barge, and row yourself to the sword, and take it and the scabbard with you, and I will ask my gift when I see my time. So Sir Arthur and Merlin alighted and tied their horses to two trees, and so they went into the ship, and when they came to the sword that the hand held, Sir Arthur took it up by the handles, and took it with him, and the arm and the hand went under the water.

RAISING READERS

Books Build Bright Futures

Dear Reader,

We'd love your attention for one more page to tell you about the crisis in children's reading, and what we can all do.

Studies have shown that reading for fun is the **single biggest predictor of a child's future life chances** – more than family circumstance, parents' educational background or income. It improves academic results, mental health, wealth, communication skills, ambition and happiness.[1]

The number of children reading for fun is in rapid decline. Young people have a lot of competition for their time. In 2024, 1 in 10 children and young people in the UK aged 5 to 18 did not own a single book at home.[2]

Hachette works extensively with schools, libraries and literacy charities, but here are some ways we can all raise more readers:

- Reading to children for just 10 minutes a day makes a difference
- Don't give up if children aren't regular readers – there will be books for them!
- Visit bookshops and libraries to get recommendations
- Encourage them to listen to audiobooks
- Support school libraries
- Give books as gifts

There's a lot more information about how to encourage children to read on our website: **www.RaisingReaders.co.uk**

Thank you for reading.

hachette LIVRE

---

[1] OECD, '21st-Century Readers: Developing Literacy Skills in a Digital World', 2021, https://www.oecd.org/en/publications/21st-century-readers_a83d84cb-en.html

[2] National Literacy Trust, 'Book Ownership in 2024'. November 2024, https://literacytrust.org.uk/research-services/research-reports/book-ownership-in-2024